SILENT TREATMENT

AND OTHER STORIES

MORRIS HERSHMAN

I0566456

THE BORGO PRESS

MMXIII

SILENT TREATMENT

FIRST EDITION

Published by Wildside Press LLC

www.wildsidebooks.com

Borgo Press Books by MORRIS HERSHMAN/LIONEL WEBB

The Blackbirder
A Knife for My Love and Further Mayhem
Rogue Slave
Sebastian
Seeing Is Deceiving: A Gail Brevard Mystery
Silent Treatment and Other Stories
Sparhawk
Stop at Nothing: Classic Crime Stories
Vicious Circles: Classic Crime Stories

SILENT TREATMENT

Tom and Ed are looking to get laid on this sultry summer night, but neither of them has much luck until they meet an acquaintance, little Harry, a man with an obnoxious body odor, small physique, and evil mind. Harry makes them a proposition: if they'll play along with him, he can guarantee that they'll pick up—and use—and abuse—a pretty girl, and she won't be able to do anything about it legally. His one condition: he's the only one who'll be doing the talking

They agree, and soon find Marsha waiting at a bus stop. They take her to a secluded park, and let her blab on about herself—and gradually become increasingly frightened as she gets no response. Harry and Tom and Ed just sit there, until the SILENT TREATMENT does its nefarious work. Seven thrilling stories torn from the pulp magazines of the 1950s and '60s!

SILENT TREATMENT

CONTENTS

THE ADVENTURE OF
THE DEVIL'S FATHER
A SHERLOCK HOLMES TALE

Fame, as my friend Mr. Sherlock Holmes occasionally insisted, is the destroyer of function. Let a man be recognized among the general public, Holmes might add pensively, and it promptly becomes impossible to proceed about his business, particularly that of pursing the craft of detection, a fate which for his part he claimed he owed entirely to the accounts which I had indited about certain of his cases.

Holmes happened to be holding forth in this vein on a chill pre-Christmas afternoon at our quarters in Baker Street when he suddenly halted himself almost in mid-sentence.

"I can relieve your mind, Watson, by informing you that the man you expect to join us will be arriving very shortly."

"Holmes, is this black magic on your part? How could you possibly know what is on my mind?"

"It is absurdly elementary, my dear fellow. You are continually looking at the door and then examining the face of the turnip watch you wear."

"Could I not be expecting a woman to join us?"

"In that case, you would be dressed far more like a bird showing off its plumage."

"And how do you know what the man will arrive 'very shortly'?"

"Because a glance out the window shows a florid-faced and worried-looking gentleman (with much military experience in his past, I'll be bound!), halting before our premises and looking at the exterior. Someday I must compose a monograph about the effects of anticipation on the reasoning processes."

Before I could apologize for not having spoken about the impending visitation, Mrs. Hudson, our landlady, was ushering a new arrival into our premises.

I said, "This is Colonel Phineas Warburton, late of Her Majesty's Service, whom I knew in Afghanistan." Indeed, he had been among the first to reach me when that infernal jezail bullet I still carry had penetrated my flesh. "We recently encounter each other in the Strand, and he asked to consult you."

"Let us hope that your problem is of interest, Colonel Warburton. Pray be seated and make your statement."

"I'll get right to the point. I have a son, Mr. Holmes, adopted as a baby by my late wife and myself shortly before a fever carried her off. I was left to raise Trevor, but my duty so occupied me that I couldn't be the best of fathers. Trevor, in a sense, raised himself."

"An elder's duty has warped more children than the basest of crimes," Holmes observed. "Please continue, Colonel."

"Trevor married and was soon in need of funds. No part of my pension would have sufficed to help. Not long after his marriage to Violet, I was horrified to learn that my son had illegally invaded the premises of a jeweler in Hatton Gardens to commit theft. With his revolver he fired at a drawer containing valuables and opened it."

"Mr. Trevor Warburton's impatience could dispose him toward further violence."

"It is that possibility, Mr. Holmes, which brings me to ask for help. You see, Trevor was captured and convicted for his crime. He is to be released from Dartmoor on a day not yet determined, but within the week, and has written me that he intends returning to Surrey."

"Where, I presume, he has lived with his wife."

"They rent a cottage in the village of Casshire."

"And you feel that he may be tempted once again into the commission of a crime."

"Tempted into violence is how I must put it. Trevor has previously written that he feels strongly about an extravagant wife having argued him into taking draconian measures to support her. It grieves and shames me to say that I greatly fear possible consequences of his anger at Violet, whether or not justified. He might perpetrate an even greater—ah, indiscretion, than in the past."

"Hm! I must tell you, sir, that I appreciate the difficulty but am not aware of any way in which I might help."

"I dreaded as much, Mr. Holmes, but there may be one solution to this hellish difficulty. If my son is told by so famous a man as Mr. Sherlock Holmes that he will be watched as closely as a dealer in a gambling hell to prevent any misstep, it may be enough to keep Trevor law-abiding from then on."

Holmes looked displeased. "It is not gratifying to confront a commission in which my façade as pictured by Watson, is wanted rather than my hard-won skills as a consulting investigator. You will be aware, though, Colonel, that I can be strongly moved by the task of preventing crime."

"You will not find me ungrateful for your help, Holmes."

"Our good landlady, Mrs. Hudson, will certainly be pleased to hear as much," Holmes said drily, rising. "I take it that you remain in London at least till the matter can be apparently resolved. Where can you be reached? The Albany? Capital."

Holmes spent the balance of daylight hours wrapped in thick coils of silence, rather than bestirring himself to arrange a prison interview with Warburton's devil of a son. He sat staring wordlessly at our bullet-pocked walls, his eyes half-shut, an unlighted meerschaum planted between his lips.

I said peevishly, "Sitting immobile for hours will not prevent a woman's being battered or, worse, murdered."

"Without evidence of the means to procure it, I do not yet know how to proceed."

Aware that I was on the threshold of an argument

at a difficult time, I descended instead to the street to take the wintry London evening air. Returning not long after, I was surprised to see Mrs. Hudson near the stairs, evidently awaiting me.

"Mr. Holmes told me to let you know that he has left until tomorrow midday, Doctor."

At least Holmes was about to give that wicked young Warburton the sort of talking to that had been richly earned. Holmes was not too late to prevent a horrid crime.

He did no reappear into the breakfast hour. A telegram from Warburton was delivered, inquiring about the current status of the matter he had placed before us. After some thought, I wrote out a telegram to the effect that all was proceeding satisfactorily. Having signed my friend's name to the concoction, I requested our page-boy to drop it off at the appropriate location.

As for the remainder of that morning and early afternoon, I hardly recall it. The fire was burning in our grate, adding warmth to the winter day, and I very much fear I dozed off. Suffice it to say that I knew nothing more until my ears made out a sound nearby and I forced both eyes open.

"Just a moment, my good man," I snapped to the scruffy stranger who had invaded our quarters. "Did you receive an appointment to meet with Mr. Holmes at this time?"

Whereupon I was astonished to hear a familiar chuckle issuing from that tearaway's parched lips.

"You are ever loyal, Watson, the blessed British

bulldog to the life," said Sherlock Holmes. "The blame for my *outré* wardrobe lies at your door, you having published such accounts of my work as to make it far more difficult for me to accomplish in everyday clothes, as I have often explained.

"Spare me, Holmes."

"To business, then. I was unable to visit Dartmoor, the trains to that area not running because of the recent snow and the current icy weather."

"What have you been doing?"

"I was able to hie myself to Surrey and the village of Casshire, where I repaired to the 'Pipe and Shag,' as the local is rather felicitously named."

"Ah! You wanted to question various residents without seeming to do so."

"Bravo, Watson! Your capacity for logical deduction grows apace, I am happy to hear. Yes, in my disguise, it seemed to me that the natives would talkl easily about young Warburton. I found several who were happy to indulge in that supposedly feminine sport of gossip. It seems that the young Warburtons—Trevor had not yet returned, I was assured—had fared badly as far as obtaining the needful was concerned. The young man attempted to find means of honest employment in London and elsewhere, but was thwarted at every turn. He had made application to serve in Her Majesty's forces when the crime took place with its grim aftermath."

"How has Mrs. Warburton lived while her husband was detained at Her Majesty's pleasure?"

"There, Watson, you put an unerring finger on a point of great interest. It would appear that Mrs. Warburton has inherited money from her late mother's will. An adequate stipend for two will shortly be arriving on the first of the month and into the foreseeable future."

"One hopes it will be enough to save her from possible unpleasantness at her husband's hands," I said. "He has been imprisoned while she, at liberty, has a newly-gained income. Is it possible he feels no regrets? That he can persuade himself she was not to blame? Is it possible? Is it likely?"

"I have taken a step to prevent the worst, if only a small step," Holmes responded. "After an overnight stay in Surrey, I met with Violet Warburton, introducing myself correctly. She understood the necessity for my garish costume without referring to it, a young woman who thinks before speaking. Cautious, obviously, with no bent for risk, which may be quite fortunate in the situation that confronts us."

"Did you tell her of the possible difficulty?"

"I did indeed. Violet Warburton loyally refuses to believe that her husband committed the crime for which he was detained, or that he might do her some mischief. She was familiar with my reputation, so she gave me her word that she would be cautious in dealing with her husband and to allow no stranger into her home for the near future. She promised to inform the local constabulary with no delay if any difficulty occurs along those lines. As the trait of caution is part of the young woman's disposition, I accept her word."

"In other words," I said, suddenly triumphant, despite the current strains, "she was familiar with your reputation which enabled you to gain her consent, because of the 'sensational' accounts I have caused to be published about your man achievements."

"A touch, Watson, distinctly a touch!" My friend's hearty chuckle was lost in the search for a stubby pen and paper on his cluttered desk. "I am writing to the principal warder of Dartmoor, a bit belatedly, asking when Trevor Warburton is to be released. Then, my dear Watson, you and I will take a hand in the game."

In the next hours Holmes beguiled himself by adding cuttings from the newspapers to his various volumes about criminal cases in the length and breadth of the Empire. This chose concluded, he favored me with several sentimental German Christmas *lieder* skillfully rendered on his violin. I was breathing deeply in pleasure when a reply came to his recent telegram. Holmes was suddenly galvanized.

"Trevor Warburton was released from Dartmoor early this morning."

"He will have returned to his wife before you can warn him to restrain further violent impulses!"

"An immediate trip must be made to Casshire. It is dark now and dirty deeds blend invisibly into the sheath of darkness." He reached for a timetable. "Dress quickly, Watson! Your company will keep strangers from noticing my undisguised presence."

"Shall I take a revolver?"

"There is less chance of mishap if we bring sticks,

and I expect further assistance from the full moon."

Our train was approaching the snow-topped chalk downs of Surrey before it occurred to me to regret that my army friend had not been asked to join us. I said as much.

"There is no reason to think that the colonel would like what he might have to witness, Watson. In this matter, even if in no other, circumstances may have conspired for the best."

My further desultory efforts at conversation were met with silence, Holmes straining to see through the once-spotless windows at our sides. He jumped to his feet shortly after we saw through our windows the ice-tipped River Way looking like a blue knife in a *blanc mange*. I joined him as the train let us off in the appropriate village, which was no different in external appearance from many others I had seen.

"The local will serve as a rough compass needle pointing north." So saying, he set off down the High Street, stick at the ready, and eyes squinting straight ahead. I found myself several steps behind, no matter how hard I struggled to catch up.

Despite my having been of assistance to him—or perhaps I flatter myself—in a number of cases, I never did become used to the lightning quickness with which my friend could act. When he whirled about to urge me by a gesture to walk more silently, I was so taken by surprise, that several seconds passed before I was able to do his bidding. I was at my usual two-three paces behind when he halted and raised one hand to keep me from moving straight ahead.

"Behind that tree," he whispered.

Holmes' face was hard, as if contemplating an enemy, eyes narrowed, lips taut against each other. Most surprising of all, he had gripped his stick so tightly that the moon's light gave those taut knuckles a semblance of fury.

"Do you think that Trevor Warburton has arrived?" I asked, careful to keep my voice low.

"No," Holmes returned. "Every room but the parlor is dark, and those who live alone are proverbially sparing of light."

The full moon shortly enabled me to see a male approaching the Warburton door, his back toward us. Warburton's devil of an adopted son, I felt sure, was walking along grounds he knew. A sturdy devil, he looked.

I turned to Holmes for guidance and received a shock when he pointed firmly back to the unfolding drama before us. A woman's footsteps eagerly approached the other side of the door as the new arrival knocked imperiously.

There was a pause, and then along the brisk night air, it was possible to hear a slurred and almost gravelly voice.

"It is I, Trevor."

No movement could be heard from the other side of the door.

Holmes, already in motion, called back to me, "Now, Watson!"

Even as Homes raced to the door, myself only a step back, Trevor Warburton's body thundered against it, striking at the correct angle to force it open. He had shown a devastating lack of caution by not hearing or paying attention to Holmes. The full moon let a cone of light over his broad back into the large room.

Holmes had raised the stick and connected solidly with the man's form. The man grunted and showed a revolver which was promptly knocked out of his nerveless hand. He suddenly staggered, having taken a total of ten steps into the room, then fell back to the floor.

Only now that Holmes had prevailed did I turn to the woman. Blood marked a cheek where she had surely been struck in the seconds that the villain had been able to do what he wished. She was pluckily recovering her balance before I started to attend her.

That done, I looked down at the monster writhing at our feet and received one of the most profound shocks of my life. For I was staring not at the youthful Trevor Warburton, but at Trevor's adopted father, my army friend, Colonel Phineas Warburton.

* * * * * * *

"The criminal himself made me suspicious of his villainy," Holmes observed on the morning train back to London. "In speaking to us at Baker Street, he offered a jarring simile about a dealer in a gambling hell, you recall, while discussing a matter in which the prime factor was a lack of money. It caused me to view other aspects of his story in a different light, and to wonder whether he himself was afflicted with a shortage of the necessary."

"And he was?"

"Indeed, yes. I was able to learn the truth in the briefest time by making contact with my brother, whose acquaintance you have made over the years. To a far greater extent than myself, Mycroft knows everything about potential scandals of any interest. Truly, he is the *Debrett's* of the disreputable. He provided me with the information that Warburton had been on the ropes, financially, for quite a while, and staving off discovery by the skin of his teeth."

"I can hardly believe that Phineas Warburton acquired gambling debts that drove him to steal his son's revolver some years ago and commit a robbery, then say nothing when Trevor was sent to prison in his stead."

"The colonel's confession freely given, even boast-fully given for some reason, must force you to accept those facts, Watson, as well as the horror that followed. Learning that his daughter-in-law had inherited enough to solve his difficulty he decided to take that money for himself by lying, cheating, and committing a base murder which could involve exposing another human being to a judicial sentence of hanging."

I nodded sadly, well aware from his jaunty confession that Phineas Warburton had lied, among other things, about Trevor's feelings for his young wife. Later, he had urged Trevor to spend a few restful hours in London upon his release from imprisonment, promising to telegraph Violet Warburton with the good news that her husband was free. Of course he had done nothing of the sort.

When the young man finally rested, the colonel felt able to wreak fatal mischief that would be laid at the door of the luckless younger man. If Mrs. Warburton hadn't failed to accept the colonel's claim of identity as Trevor in those last moments, he would have been entirely successful, thus inheriting the dead daughter-in-law's money from Trevor's estate after the latter had been hanged.

Couldn't he have thrown himself at the mercy of the young people and borrowed a considerable portion of the money that he needed?"

"He lacked enough judgment to consider doing so." Holmes tapped his own forehead as if to say that the man's faculties had been impaired by greed.

"I fear, after having seen him, that the matter may be more tragic than you believe, Holmes. Warburton's reason may have been shaken to the foundations by his many reverses, and he may never leave an institution for the—the insane."

"Your apprehensions could be wholly justified, Watson, but Warburton's stay cannot be without an end. Everything in this span of our lives is *pro tempore*, old fellow, for we begin afresh after we leave this first plane of existence."

[("*I introduced to his notice) the problem of Colonel Warburton's madness.*"]—A. Conan Doyle, "The Adventure of the Engineer's Thumb."

SILENT TREATMENT

They were sitting together at one of the tables in the bar. Harry scowled out the plate glass window. Somebody had left a greasy thumbprint in one corner, but Harry ignored that.

"It's summer and pretty girls are walking down the streets, and we sit here and do nothing. You know why?"

Tom Abbot said, "No money."

"That's not *my* reason."

It was early evening and girls passed by, their faces and figures illuminated by neon lights outside and above them. Whenever a girl passed, attractive or not, Harry's little eyes would drop down to her flanks.

"A guy needs money and a car, but mainly a girl who's willing to let him play around. Right?"

"Let's not make a Federal case out of it," Tom Abbot said tiredly. At his left, somewhere in the mellow darkness, a singing voice, distorted by a loudspeaker, boomed out of a juke box; varicolored lights snaked down along his sides, hurting his eyes when they ranged that way.

"For a guy like me," Harry said doggedly, "the girls

aren't willing. I'm short and damn near bald, and I don't make so much loot that the women fall all over themselves to get near me. But I want a woman tonight, and I'm damn well gonna get one."

Tom pulled his hair back against his forehead with the flat of a hand. Seeing Harry's little eyes narrowing venomously at the gesture, Tom set down his hand to circle the glass of beer in front of him, instead.

"I don't like professionals," he said shortly, wincing at the very notion of "professionals."

"Neither do I. Sick and tired 'em. I go once a week, sure, but what the hell! I'm a man!"

"No professionals for me tonight," Tom smiled. "Or any other night."

"We don't need 'em." Harry leaned forward. He rubbed his hands against each other. "I've got an idea, a big idea."

Tom shook his head. "Include me out," he said quickly, "if you've got rape on the brain."

"No rape." Harry finished his shot glass and wiped the sides of his mouth with an initialed handkerchief. "My idea is that we pick up a girl and get what we want and can't be charged with any crime."

Tom said faintly. "Sure, you dream about the girl. You pick her up in your head." He tapped his forehead with an index finger. "Besides, if it's such a great idea, why don't you do it by yourself?"

"I can't manage it by myself." Harry finally set down his glass on the cardboard circle and belched without covering up his mouth. "What do you say?"

"Tell me how you'd do it."

"No, not till we've got her," Harry said sharply. "If I don't play that way, when the time comes, you might double-cross me. I can't fight for what's mine, and nobody in the world gives a damn for what I'm entitled to."

Tom Abbott shrugged helplessly. To cover his brief confusion, he drew out a cigar from an inside pocket. While trying to light it, he looked little Harry up and down, taking in the shabby clothes and frayed collar, the neutral shirt with a stain between the third and fourth buttons, the jacket that was too long for him.

"I'm not willing to go into anything blind," he said finally.

"Interested, though, I can see." Harry chuckled. "I'll make you a proposition. If I can get Ed Land to go into it blind, on my say-so, will you come in, too?"

Tom said, surprised, "Ed Land? Three men in this? Is that what you want?"

"Three is the right number for this idea because...." Harry looked down at himself, and a flush spread over his sun-brown cheeks. "I can keep in the background until just before we do it. Well, do we try to find Ed Land and talk to him?"

Tom glanced at his watch. It was seven o'clock of a summer's night, the kind that drags on forever, or so it seems. He had no intention of getting mixed up in a wild scheme, but there'd be no harm in following it through for a while.

"If you can get Ed to agree," he said, "I—I'll think

it over."

"Let's get a move on, then."

Outside the air-conditioned bar, heat struck at them with renewed fury. Little Harry, in unbuttoning his shirt at the neck, cracked a small white button in half. His eyes admired every tall woman who passed, and often his head would turn. Tom talked as little as possible and found himself looking straight ahead or glancing to his side at store windows.

They found Ed Land in front of a nearby liquor store, polishing the sides of his yellow convertible in the blue-green light from the store's interior. When Harry called out Ed Land's name, the man turned and nodded. He was sweating freely, pearls trickling off the edges of his blond hair. He swabbed at them, then pointed at the car.

"Damn thing is always dirty," he said, then looked down at Harry. "What's on your little mind tonight?... no, I've got a date a little later on, but I'm not getting any action out of the girl...you're crazy to think I'd come in on anything like that."

Ed Land lowered his voice in response to Harry's urgent gestures. He wiped at his forehead, trying to calm himself. He looked up uneasily at Tom, who was standing off to one side, hands in his pockets and glancing at the owner of the liquor store sitting in front of the place on a folding chair and trying to do a cross-word puzzle in a paper.

"Besides, it's a hell of a risk," Ed Land added. "I can get all the girls I want without having to take a chance on spending the next twenty years upstate."

"Suit yourself," Harry said, almost casually. "But this'd be a good night for it, especially when you can't get into any trouble if you do what I tell you."

Ed Land and Tom Abbott exchanged glances, then Ed looked down at his sweaty shirt and at his car.

"Like I was telling Tom here," Harry said slowly, "I know you guys wouldn't want to have me along on a pitch like this, and if I tell you how to do it you might get rid of me. It's nothing personal, I guess, just that I'm so short, I'm a freak."

Ed Land flushed. Tom looked down steadily at Harry.

"You wouldn't hurt the girl afterwards," Tom said cautiously. Ed Land showed surprise.

"Kill her, you mean?" Harry chuckled, his breath rolling around Tom's belly; Tom felt the hot wind and took a step back. "We don't have to. In fact, the thing we're going to do, it can't be called rape at all."

"You'll want to use this." Ed Land leaned over and an extended knuckle touched a side of the car. "The girl can identify it later on."

"But she won't do it in court." Harry clapped his small hands together, as if for attention. "Do you know why not? Because she's going to ask us to do it to her. Get that straight, she'll be willing."

"Do you mean that any girl we pick up—?" Ed Land grinned down at Harry. "That's something I've got to see!" He brought down a large hand on top of Harry's head. "You're one smart little runt if you can manage it."

"then you're in." Harry turned quickly to Tom Abbott. "And you too, Tom, right?"

Was it a kind of hysteria?

Two men responded to the leading of an evil little man, nodding on cue. Harry seemed to take special pleasure in forcing the two normal-sized men to lean forward and bend down their heads so that they could listen more easily.

Their attitudes to each other had changed, too. Tom Abbott and Ed Land looked distrustful, and their eyes, whenever possible, avoided the sight of little Harry.

"All you two have to do," Harry said, "is to persuade a girl to get into the car and drive to some lonely section. That's all. And once the girl is in the car, let me do the talking."

"You?" Ed suddenly covered his lips, probably to force back a smile.

"It's very important," Harry snapped. "If you boys talk to her or even to each other, I won't be responsible for what happens." The beady little eyes rested on Ed Land, then lingered on Tom Abbott. "And if I keep quiet, nobody says anything. Is that clear?"

The three of them stepped into the car. Ed Land muttered under his breath. Harry took the front seat next to him and signaled Tom Abbott to sit beside them.

"We'll find a girl, to start with."

His eyes rested on most of them, thin, fat, short, tall. Especially the tall ones, of course. Tom was aware of the little man's body odor and drew a heavy breath.

Twice he turned to face Ed Land, but said nothing.

"There," Harry said suddenly. "She's it. The one at the bus stop."

"No, not that one," Tom Abbott said it automatically, the words darting out of his mouth. He had never seen the girl before. He sat back, flushing.

"What's the matter? Do you think she looks too innocent?" Harry grinned. "She's the one. I've made up my mind."

The girl stood in front of the Bus Stop sign, a tall redhead with clear skin and thin lips. She wore a print dress. Her shoulder strap purse swung back and forth gently. Harry, staring at her, breathed harder than usual, then forced himself to look away.

The car pulled up near the sign.

"Like a ride, Miss?" Ed Land asked pleasantly. "By the time a bus comes along, a girl could turn old and gray with seventeen kids."

"No, thanks."

Harry folded his hands in his lap and began staring at Tom Abbott. Tom turned, looked up at the girl.

"We just want a little company for a few blocks, Miss."

The girl glanced at Ed Land, then at Tom Abbott, then at Harry. At the sight of Harry, a smile quirked the edges of her lips. She shrugged.

"Well, I've been waiting for about half an hour. I just live a dozen blocks over. Garden Street. 162 Garden...I hope it isn't out of your way."

"Of course not, Miss," Ed Land said.

Tom Abbott stepped out of the car and pulled his former seat forward so that the girl could edge into the back. She did it carefully, bent over, the shoulder strap purse swinging wildly. When Tom seated himself in the car again, his nostrils twitched at the whiff of her perfume.

It was possible for Tom, sitting where he did, to see the girl's face reflected in the driver's mirror. She sat a little stiffly at first, then pushed back her shoulder against the cushions. No one talked. She smiled again.

"I haven't met the third one. He hasn't even talked to me."

Ed Land tapped Harry's arm with an elbow. "Introduce yourself to the lady," he said.

Harry glared back, crossing a forefinger against his lips for silence. Then he sat impassively, hands folded in his lap.

Streets passed by them, and lighted sections gave way to those with dim lighting, and then to streets that often weren't lit at all.

"I said," the girl repeated, "I haven't met...come to think of it, I don't know who any of you are."

Seen through the driver's mirror, she smiled again, then shrugged it away. She was glancing out the window and talking; steam appeared on the glass.

"I'm surprised that three men like yourselves would be shy with one girl."

This time it was Harry who smiled. In fact he put up a hand to his lips, probably to keep from snickering or laughing. Ed Land drove stiffly. Tom was impassive, but his hands were fisted in his pockets.

"My name's Marsha Finley. I'm a secretary. There! Does that help to break the ice?"

Tom turned his head briefly, but Harry glared till he resumed his former position. Harry's body odor had become intensified from the moment the girl had stepped into the car.

"I think I'll open a window if you all don't mind."

The girl fumbled briefly with the window handle. Gusts of warm air drifted to the front.

"I swear I don't know what's the matter with you men. I never saw people so shy...you're going the wrong way! Garden Street is at the right."

She leaned forward. Her soft, short-nailed fingers touched Ed Land's left shoulder, briefly depressing some of the padding.

"I said that Garden Street is over the other way. Didn't you hear me?"

Her face was a little whiter, especially around the lips. When she sat back, though, shadows reappeared under her eyes.

"Where are you taking me?" Her voice was so much lower that it was hard to hear. "What do you want with me? Just because I agreed to a car ride, that doesn't mean...I'm a good girl. I'm a good girl."

She repeated that twice more, looking up briefly to see if any impression had been made.

"Is this a joke of some kind?" She sounded relieved. "Of course it is. You're trying to scare me, that's all. Well, it won't work. I don't scare so easy."

Tom was wiping his hands against the sides of his pants. Ed Land frowned fiercely as he drove. Harry's lips were extended at the corners, hinting at a smile.

They reached a wooded park area. A muddy-looking line of water softened the smell of animal droppings. Along the route, cracking old wooden benches were spaced awkwardly. Grass, growing wild, bent to occasional wind whispers.

"All right now, you've had your joke and I'm going."

Harry's body odor was almost unbearable. Even Ed Land darted small glances over towards him. Tom stared at the mirror, which showed the girl looking determinedly at the car doors. Suddenly she leaned back.

"No, you'll stop me, won't you? If you've gone this far, you won't let me out."

Marsha Finley was probably trying not to show fright. Her large eyes were wide, though, the brows quirked, and her hands shaky against her sides.

"What do you want?"

A shout this time. Ed Land looked uneasily at Tom and at little Harry. It was 9:30, Tom saw with blearily surprised eyes. It had been a full hour ago that the girl had stepped into the car.

"All right, if you won't talk, I won't talk, either. You just want to get me nervous, that's all. We can sit here and wait till doomsday."

She folded her hands and set them down in her lap.

Water bubbled nearby. A car streaked past, and musical notes hung briefly in the air. The wistful look in the girl's face as she stared out the window at the passing car, brought a flush to Rom Abbott's cheeks. Time and again he opened his mouth, hesitated, then snapped it shut. Silence was hurting not only the girl's nerves, but his own. He could hear the tick of his wrist watch, and feel suddenly cold metal against the underside of his wrist.

Ed Land squirmed in his seat. Harry hadn't moved since the car had been stopped.

At ten o'clock, the girl said suddenly, tiredly, "Get it over with. Whatever you want, please get it over with. I can't stand this." And again, "Please get it over with. Please."

Tom caught at his lower lip, forcing back words. He could sense food churning his stomach and rising to the border of his throat. Ed Land lowered his eyes. Harry darted looks of triumph at the two others. When he suddenly spoke, Tom had to cover his mouth to keep from calling out with shock.

"Let's understand something, baby," Harry's voice was surprisingly clear. "We're not *forcing* you to have a little fun with us, right?"

"I—I—"

"That isn't wrong, baby, is it? We won't make a move unless you tell us you want us to. Do you want us to?"

In these conditions, she couldn't say no. That was little Harry's big plan, to pressure a girl into saying she wanted it.

Tom pounded his fists against his kneecaps. Ed Land was white-faced.

Twice Harry had to repeat the question. The girl didn't answer. He was quiet, folding his hands and waiting.

Marsha Finley sighed. "Whatever you say. I can't stand this."

Total abject surrender; but Harry wasn't satisfied.

"Like I told you, baby, if you say no, then none of us will put a glove on you. Would you want some action with us?"

"If I say no, will you let me out of here?"

Silence.

Marsha said tautly, "Please, let's get it over with so that I can go. Please, please, I'll do anything you say."

Harry said, "Sure you will, baby." Quickly he set one foot on the seat, which caused such weight on it as he lifted himself that Tom was thrown off-balance.

Probably it was the last straw. Tom reached out a hand across the little man's chest.

"Keep away from her, you damn freak!"

Harry struck back sharply with the first two fingers of his right hand against Tom's throat. Tom fell back and carried the little man with him. His hands found Harry's throat, and he could feel arm muscles tensing as he used them. Breath passed between his fingers at first, then nothing.

Harry lay against the seat, his eyes open, fist closed. Ed Land, looking down, shuddered.

"Disgusting little creep," Ed Land said. "Disgusting."

He bunched spittle back of his lips, but paused and suddenly turned, then opened the car window and spat outside, instead.

Tom Abbott and Ed Land looked at each other, then at the girl. Her heightened pallor, her helplessness, brought pain throbbing to Tom's chest.

"Do you want *us*," he asked the girl, "to go back there to you?"

"I—I, no." At the silence she added, "I thought you two were all right, but I suppose you won't let it pass by. You win. You win. I want you to—want you to...."

Tom stepped out the door and pulled forward his former seat, then stepped cautiously into the back. Ed Land sighed, drew out a scout knife he always carried and settled down to cleaning dirt from his fingernails till his turn would come.

CHOICE OF WEAPONS

Harris Kyle set his two trim suitcases down against a sagging palm tree which seemed to be growing out of the cracked old pavement. With a clean folded handkerchief he tapped his narrow forehead, his thin cheeks and the receding upper lip at the point where the bureau chief had pointed disdainfully to a burgeoning mustache and then ordered him to shave the damn thing off.

"You're the wrong type to hide anything, even your upper lip," the chief added in puzzled tones. "You're nothing but a good inside man—fine with paper clips and inter-office memoranda and nothing else. That's how come I'll never know why Jed Morgan put through a request to have you help on his current assignment."

"I—I think I can understand that," Kyle said as soon as he could get back his poise. "He probably wants somebody on hand who is efficient and thorough."

The chief nodded reluctantly. "Seems like it, I'm afraid. Do you really want to go out to the French West Indies? I warn you; anything involving the local commies anywhere has got some danger in it."

"I'll be careful, Chief. I always am."

He had watched the chief shrug in a baffled way and then agree to let him go. Now that Kyle was here, however, he muttered at the warm, moist air so close to the harbor of this sweltering city called Fort-de-France. A nearby tourist grunted something to his wife about a town called Three Islands and about Josephine Bonaparte. Kyle shrugged and proceeded to his business.

The street swarmed with men and women who wanted cabs, but it was Kyle who managed to get the first one that was clear. He gave his destination briefly, then looked out of a window long enough to register the fact that the women were wearing cheap cotton print dresses and that the buildings were painted yellow, with balconies to match.

Once Kyle had mentally noted those points, he leaned forward in his seat as if to help the driver get to where he wanted to go.

He registered at the small hotel just off the Lido Road and checked that his hotel room was equipped with the basic needs.

In order to appear more like a tourist, he changed into sports slacks and a slim-at-the-midriff sports shirt. He placed the strap of his Zeiss-Ikonta camera case meticulously on his left shoulder, and reached the lobby with minutes to spare. As he might have known, considering that he had to deal with a free-and-easy type like Jed Morgan, he was early.

After twenty minutes of waiting, he walked across the massive lobby. A cinnamon-skinned clerk eyed him appreciatively, then smiled.

"Do you know a Mr.—?" Kyle started, then swallowed and made up his mind to be more round-about. He fumbled a few words, though, before giving it up and walking away.

The clerk quietly made a phone call, then nodded warily in Kyle's direction a few moments later when a couple of dark-skinned men walked into the lobby. The men said nothing, but Kyle noticed furtive glances directed at him.

He was paged not too long afterward. The phone was placed on a stand between vases of hibiscus and anthurium flowers, at which distractions Kyle glared with a complete lack of approval.

"Don't mention any names," the voice of Jed Morgan came through affably at the other end of the phone." I think you'd like to rent a car and have dinner in about an hour at a restaurant called *L'Auberge du Manoir*. You should have no trouble finding the place."

"I'm sure I'll manage," Kyle said.

"Oh, by the way, have you got a gun?" Jed asked.

"A Beretta nine-fifty B," Kyle said proudly.

"Bring it along," Jed Morgan said, as if asking for a cough drop. "And put it in a gift box, will you? Tie a ribbon on it, too. Don't forget. See you later.

Flabbergasted as he was by such ridiculous instructions, Kyle proceeded to follow them. A taxi took him downtown, where a huge body of water meandered lazily through the business district. Kyle was still shaking his head over that particular un-businesslike phenomenon when he reached the *garage américaine*. In this town, he decided, it would be easier to find repair parts for a *Dauphine* than for any American car, so he rented one.

It took him several minutes of shrewd driving to lose the tough guys who had been following him in a beaten-up car of their own.

At a gift shop in the *Rue Schölcher* he arranged to have the Beretta wrapped in a fancy way. While the packaging went on, he glanced down the street at the yellow-tinted outside of a movie theatre advertising a dubbed-in-French version of a Hollywood Western.

He drove past the eating place, *L'Auberge du Manoir*, and then decided that it would be safe for him to go in. With the package under one arm, he walked determinedly into the darkened interior of the place.

Jed Morgan was sitting comfortably at a table in the far corner, his pudding-face shiny as he talked to a girl. He gave a lazy smile when he saw Kyle, then gestured him over with a soft hand and introduced him to the girl.

"Armine, this is Harris Ky—"

"Get her out," Kyle said brusquely. "We have to talk."

"Armine is a personal friend," Jed told him. "By the way, did you bring that gift I asked for?"

Kyle threw the gift-wrapped Beretta down on the table in a silent rebuke at Jed's having been too engrossed with his companion to see it for himself. He turned to the girl.

"May I ask you to please leave, young lady?" he snapped. "You've had it."

Armine, an attractive brown-eyed blonde whose figure wasn't entirely hidden by a colored dress, made a point of folding her hands adamantly and putting them down on the table.

"If she won't leave," Kyle said, "then I will."

"Really?" Jed took a bite of conch from his plate, then a bite of stewed octopus, and finally a bite of fricasseed raccoon. Then he started all over again on the conch. To the girl he said, "Eat your cod in pepper sauce, Armine. It's good for you.

Kyle turned on his heels and walked to his car. Jed Morgan followed, carrying one glass of light rum and one glass of dark rum in each soft hand. As soon as Jed sat down in the car, Kyle spilled the contents of each glass out the window. Lines of pain briefly appeared on Jed's round face.

"The *vieil acajou* I don't mind," he said, gesturing to the glass that had held the dark rum. "The *jeune* I do mind—oh, about the girt you were nice enough to bring. I left it for Armine, you know. It was intended for her."

"You gave her that gun?" Kyle drew a deep breath to keep from exploding. "Do you think I came out here and gave you a government issue Beretta to give to some girl? That gun alone costs the government exactly—"

"You came out here to help me," Jed Morgan's voice was soft, as usual, but it quieted Kyle. "Our contact,

Octave St. Juste, is a man who infiltrated an organization of men who call themselves Communists. Actually, they're hoodlums who use the name so as to get extra help from outside the Indies."

"And I assume our contact has gotten some evidence," Kyle said. "Where is it?"

"Nobody knows that except Octave St. Juste himself. The evidence consists of a hundred sheets of ruled yellow paper that's part of a code which can be broken, and gives information on the members and their plans to take over the Martiniques first and then the rest of the Indies. His problem is to get the evidence to me."

"Why doesn't he use a police guard to take the stuff to you? That sounds pretty easy as far as I can tell."

"If he does that, then the bad guys will find out," Jud remarked with such gentleness that it didn't seem possible he was being sarcastic. "St. Juste is being watched wherever he goes; anybody he talks to is automatically under suspicion. Above all, he knows that if he takes any overt action then the couple who watch him might—well, take steps. He doesn't exactly believe in *vodun,* I understand, but doesn't want to run afoul of the *vodun* powers that be."

"Voodoo, you mean/" Kyle didn't know whether to laugh scornfully or bite his knuckles in vexation. "If that's the case, we may be here forever and I'll certainly have to change hotels. A pair of tough-looking men followed me out of the lobby and I had trouble shaking them off."

"I'm surprised they got onto you, considering how

inconspicuous you are."

Morgan patted Kyle's shoulder. "Don't let it bug you, Harry, old man."

Jed Morgan left the *Dauphine* slowly and strolled back into the restaurant in spite of Kyle's repeated efforts to call him back. Kyle finally sat against the cushions and brooded about the value of decisiveness and efficiency such as he himself had had to cultivate for years in order to get what he wanted out of such easygoing types as Morgan. There did seem to be something wrong about his theory when he came to try working it out on Jed.

Kyle was joined by the other agent in a few moments and Jed politely but firmly eased him out of the driver's seat.

"It's time you saw Diamond Rock," he said, exactly as if Kyle had come to Martinique for his health or personal pleasure.

The water at Diamond Rock was so blue that the sight of it almost hurt Kyle's city-trained eyes. He sat and fumed while Jed rented a bathing suit, and resisted all blandishments to do the same and go swimming.

Morgan eventually shrugged and left him alone there in the car.

An hour passed when Kyle spotted the girl, Armine, who had been sitting with Jed at the restaurant. Instead of being deeply impressed by her shape as displayed in a bright red-and-white swimsuit, Kyle watched balefully as she walked over to Jed, who had reappeared, and spoke to him briefly.

Jed, who was making his way back to the car, nodded and smiled at her, making what was almost certainly a flirtatious remark. He came ahead to the car at a faster pace than he generally took.

"I'll change back into civvies and be right with you," he smiled. "It looks like we're going to be in business tonight and get the papers from our friend."

Kyle's heart jumped. "How do you know for sure?"

"Armine just told me that St. Juste has agreed to pass the material over and do it in the way I suggested to her."

"If he's being guarded all the time he'll get killed," Kyle remarked disapprovingly.

Jed turned grimly serious. "That's where *you* come in, my friend. *You're* going to be the hero of the night."

Unfortunately for his peace of mind, Kyle couldn't pry any more information out of Jed, as he drove into town, talking idly about the importance to the natives of *vodun* or voodoo. When they reached Port-de-France proper, still hazy in the late afternoon sun, Jed insisted on standing Kyle to a drink at an outdoor bar. But he couldn't persuade Kyle to order anything but the familiar item which the bartender called *le ponch*.

"I'll pick you up at eight o'clock in the lobby of your hotel," Jed told him over his own *coeur de chauffe*.

Kyle, who had been disapprovingly watching steam rise from the light and strong liquid in Jed's glass, looked up in alarm. "We have to meet someplace else or you'll run into those hoods. They're certain to be in the lobby waiting for me."

"I won't mind having them around."

Kyle was jolted out of his usual purposeful efficiency. "For heaven's sake, Jed, tell me exactly what you're doing and why."

"No, Harry. You'll invent too many objections. I'd rather we just went ahead. Eight o'clock, then."

The pair of hoodlums were indeed waiting for Kyle in the hotel lobby, as he discovered on his return. He took a bath and changed into an evening suit that would have been perfect for the night hours at Miami Beach.

At precisely two minutes to eight o'clock, he was in the lobby. Jed Morgan, of course, didn't shamble inside to join him until eight-twenty. His pudding-face was lightly tanned.

"How would you like to see the Superba?" Jed asked him affably. "Quite a place, Harry. It'll make your trip complete."

Kyle whispered urgently, "You aren't going to get those papers in a public place are you? In the circumstances, that's imposs—"

"Harry, you're proving that I'm a wise man. Let's get out to the car and go."

Harris Kyle found himself in the middle of something like a New Orleans *Mardi Gras* when he stepped into the barn-like building called the Superba at ten o'clock that night. The huge room was decorated with colored streamers, paper lanterns and balloons. Creoles in costume walked back and forth, calling out to friends or laughing or singing.

"Our 'friends' are here," Kyle said promptly, having

glanced back to see that the pair of hoodlums who'd been following him had come inside.

"You shouldn't always think about business," Jed said cheerfully. "How do you like the costumes? That girl over there is dressed like Josephine Bonaparte in the *Savane* statue. That one is a *columbine*. And there's a fellow dressed as a *pierrot*. There's probably a *harlequin* not too far from—oh yes, there he is."

A knight in armor cheerfully whacked the hilt of his rubber sword over the head of a dragon as Kyle passed with Jed.

"We're too conspicuous," Kyle decided. "don't tell me I'm being pushy, Jed, when all I'm saying is that it's impossible to get those papers when we're just about the only ones who are dressed normally."

"Come on upstairs," Jed said, and smiled.

They walked up a wide carpeted staircase. Jed's eyes were on the girl in front of them, a girl wearing lace and silk, with an overskirt swept up on one side. A few more tourists were in the balcony, at tables set down on graduated levels.

A lively *béguine* was being played, and women on the dance floor moved like so many blurs of flashing color in the corner of Kyle's eyes. Kyle looked around warily, as if he expected to find traps everywhere.

A distinguished-looking man with gray hair stood up from a barstool, making it the one empty seat in the place. Jed went to it promptly and ordered *woom*, which turned out to be the creole dialect version of that popular local product, rum.

Kyle had followed Jed to the bar and looked around expectantly at every face.

"Well, where is he? How do you think you'll get—"

His right shoulder was tapped gently, and Kyle whirled around to see Armine once again. She was pushing the familiar gift-wrapped package, presumably with the Beretta inside it, toward him. Or was there something inside far more important than a gun?

"Here you are," the girl said softly. "And whatever else you do, be sure not to open it."

Rather than take instructions from the girl, Kyle turned around accusingly to Jed Morgan, who had finished his rum drink and was blotting his lips ostentatiously with a napkin.

"Don't open it," Jed told him easily, in the same casual tone with which he had described the costumes a few minutes earlier. "Armine just took that package from Octave St. Juste."

"It doesn't *feel* like there are papers inside," Kyle remarked promptly. "And besides, those hoods are coming over here right now."

"Why, yes, now you mention it," Jed smiled. "So they are."

Kyle tried to keep the package from being knocked out of his hand by one of the hoodlums, but couldn't do it. The package left his grasp and he made a fist and felt it thud into a man's face. There was a great pressure against his stomach and his sides.

Kyle was not a hero and he knew it only too well, but there are certain limits to the amount of personal indignity a chap should have to take before flailing back.

He had the sudden sick sensation of being slugged expertly, just behind the ear, and of saying some words that his maiden aunt in Worcester, Massachusetts, would have turned pale to hear.

After that, for a long moment, there was nothing.

From a distance he could hear a sudden chorus of rising murmurs, then a drum-roll just before the band launched into the strains of the *Marseillaise*. The music of the French national anthem didn't affect Kyle or any of the men who had launched the struggle against him.

Only vaguely afterwards did he remember Jed Morgan joining the fight, and then the police form the local prefecture coming into it a few minutes after that. Kyle could vividly recall seeing one of the hoodlums with the package start trying to run a zigzag course to safety and freedom.

He would have given anything in the world at that moment to have the Beretta in his hands, but Jed Morgan had indirectly taken it away from him almost on arrival.

Then there was the brief talk between Jed and *sous-lieutenant*, a spectacularly mustachioed man in his forties. The police officer finally permitted Jed to take Kyle out of there. For once in his life, the efficient Kyle had to be helped out to where he wanted to go; in this case to the *Dauphine*.

Morgan drove in a relaxed position, but the car streaked along like a knife through butter. Wind coming in by the open window was enough to bring Kyle back to consciousness of the fact that he still had no idea what was on Jed's mind.

Still groggy, Kyle said, "Where are we going?"

"Airport. We can have our things sent after us."

Kyle laughed mirthlessly. "End of a successful mission."

"Exactly."

Kyle was too wrought-up to comprehend what had just been said. "Where's the girl? Where's this fellow, St. Juste?"

"Armine probably took Octave St. Judte back to his house. The old boy needs a rest."

"He's done all that work in vain, so I suppose he really does need a rest." Kyle sighed. "I'm sorry I lost the papers, but I did the best I was able."

"You did exactly what had to be done," Jed said sincerely. "You had the important part, and you handled it perfectly."

"Don't butter me up. You won't hide that it's all been a waste of time."

"It certainly hasn't," Jed said, taking a corner on one wheel and a half. "I'm bringing the papers home. They're on me, right now."

"But that's absolutely impossible!"

"Oh no it isn't. St. Juste simply had the papers micro-filmed, then put them into a plastic case no bigger than the sort of cardboard container that holds a hundred paper clips. Then he put spirit gum on one side of the case and, holding it in his palm, went to the upstairs bar at the Superba. When he saw me coming he put the case on the underside of the barstool as he was getting up and—"

"That gray-haired man, you mean? I remember him now."

"I thought you would. Then I sat down and waited till you were distracting the hoodlums in a fight. That was when I reached down for the plastic case containing the micro-filmed papers, palmed it, put it into a pocket and did my best to get you out of the place as soon as possible."

"But what about the gift box and all the other hocus-pocus?"

"That was vital, Harry, not hocus anything. I managed to get your gun because I thought you might use it otherwise and perhaps take a human life."

Kyle flushed, but promptly covered his face to hide it.

"Then I had to take the hoods' minds off what was really happening and you helped out with that problem, Harry; with the invaluable assistance of Armine and of St. Juste himself, who picked up the package from the barman with whom Armine had left it for him. Now when the hoodlums and their bosses are arrested they'll all think it was bad *juju*, bad magic. St. Juste obviously passed nothing across to anyone."

"How can you be so sure they'll think it's bad luck after having been outsmarted by you and St. Juste?"

"Because Armine took the gun out of that gift box of yours and put it in a voodoo doll with a hatpin through its head." Jed smiled. "A sure sign of very bad luck to come. Even the more sophisticated of them half-believe in *vodun*, and I'm not actually sure there isn't something to it after all—but never mind. The point is that you came out here to save a man's life, Harry, and you did."

Harris Kyle uncovered his face and sat up a little more stiffly.

"So I'm a bloody hero," he said glumly. And, after a long pause, "Jed, a favor, please. Next time you ask me to a horse race, buy me a program so I'll know what the hell goes on. I sure didn't this time."

NEVER TOO LATE

I'm pretty sure that the thick glasses I wore as a boy not only shaped my face but changed my life. The whole town of River Walk took it as an article of faith that Alva Seymour, the pharmacist's son—known as "squint" or "four-eyes"—was a good student who paid heavily for his excellence by being a rotten athlete and clumsy with the girls. Well, it's true that I never had a highly-developed killer instinct for the school sporting events and I'd never be trusted on the basketball court or football field. But I did apply myself so that I wasn't in the worst physical shape. I had taught myself to be a smooth dancer, too, a skill which the girls appreciated from some guy who wasn't an overwhelming physical presence and thought he was dancing as if he must be back on the sporting field.

This particularly summer-like morning, on my way to Westside High School, let me tell you, though, that fourteen-year-old Alva Seymour wasn't sure of himself. I can remember looking around right and left and over both shoulders with almost every quick step I took. There happened to be some very good reasons for that much caution.

I was just turning the corner of the Happy Bee Soda Shoppe and smiling back at the owner—my dad wouldn't put a fountain into the drugstore because he felt that Joe Davies had to make a living, too—I almost ran into Elroy Thorsen, one of the battling brothers who were known as the school scourges, big, strong, and with meanness to match.

I pulled back, of course. Too far back because I bumped into Omar Thorsen, who was known as the nastier brother, a close call if ever there was one.

"You!" Omar called out and nodded grimly. "I figured the best student would be walking around here, and I really wanted to tell you that me and Elroy are tickled to be in the same classes with you."

Which was the cue for Elroy to chime in, "You're an example to us."

They were more-or-less quoting Mrs. Barrie, our civics teacher, who had praised me to the skies after rousting the Thorsens for having cut classes and ignoring homework. The youngest in the class, she had said truthfully, referring to me, was the hardest worker as well as the best student.

I didn't smile cravenly, but looked around instead. My sister was standing about half a block away and talking to one of her boy friends who I didn't know, his back toward me. No help would be coming from that direction at the time when I was in dire need.

I wouldn't give the Thorsens the satisfaction of calling for help, but turned to run. Omar, with a ham hand quick as lightning, reached up for my glasses and hurled them down to the sunny May sidewalk. I heard the glass tinkling into bits even as I hurled myself toward the curb.

My arms were caught up from behind and I was whirled around to where I'd be facing River Walk's own Darth Vader. Kicking behind me was useless, the highly-experienced Elroy having planted himself too close to me.

Before I could turn my head Omar had raised a stubby second finger and pushed it against my right eye. I did pull back just a little so that I didn't experience the full strength of his viciousness. It was impossible to see anything except dark and gray flashes or to feel anything except great pain.

Some grown man on the street called out, "Leave him alone!" but didn't come forward to help. A few others were annoyed but they only murmured their disapproval and no move was made in my direction. Everybody had reason to be aware that the Thorsens didn't take well to civics inside the classroom or out of it.

I seemed to be hearing from a distance that my sister had screamed and two sets of steps were hurrying closer to me. I felt myself being touched gently, being soothed.

Her boyfriend had already shooed the Thorsens out of our faces like they were so many midges, and I suppose they went because the guy was a stranger to them, an unknown factor. I didn't know why those two had made tracks without launching another strike, but when my sight cleared I made sense out of that. This fellow had a strong but slim body and powerful hands. He might have done plenty of damage to the scourges.

Ruth's alarmed voice was clear. "You have to go home Al," my sister was saying almost shrilly. "We'll take you there."

Meaning her boyfriend and herself. The guy had a different idea, which was very much appreciated by a kid who had no intention of becoming a cause of condescending pity from any others. "There used to be a first aid station at Westside High, and if it still exists the nurse will take care of anything that has to be done."

This fellow's easy self-confidence did a lot to settle me down, believe it or not. I was walked to school while Ruth went home to get one of my substitute pairs of thick glasses. Neighbors clustered around me now and the guy simply turned around and walked off.

The Thorsens glared at me during the school day but Al glared right back through the substitute glasses and sailed through the day's math test and the history quiz about the Korean War. I was first to finish my essay about the Siege of Dienbienphu and the lessons to be learned from it, and if you want to know I did pretty well. As usual, I have to say without modesty.

I was paying back a quarter I owed on the steps outside the front entrance at the end of the school day when some dude drew a deep breath almost in my ear. Turning around swiftly I saw Omar Thorsen coming up behind me.

"You guys disappear, all of you," he said quietly to the others. "I'm gonna take care of the best student and do it right here."

That was when Violet Jardine, who was one of the stars of my English class but needed help in science, called out, and even ran at Omar. He pushed her away. She fell, swore at him and had to be kept from being hurt.

There was no place for an effective retreat and I was reaching into a pocket as if to draw out some weapon. Just as I made that particular move, not too hopefully, Omar's features turned a lot grayer than nature had intended. Suddenly he was mad and helpless at the same time.

"Anything you want, kid?" It was the hard but silky-smooth voice of Ruth's new boyfriend. I guess he'd been on the way to see Ruth again, but stopped to find out if I was having any more trouble. I was starting to like this particular boyfriend of hers more and more.

Omar stared, silent. Elroy, his brother, started over as if to join him, but Omar made a restraining motion in that direction, and Elroy stopped with a foot already extended.

"If you want to fight him," Ruth's friend said crisply, "pick one of you to fight. He's scrappy and an even fight could surprise you."

Omar actually did carry a knife, which I didn't know till he took it out, freed a thick blade and touched one finger to it, the second finger of his right hand with which I had thought he was going to blind me.

"If you boys want to take me on at the same time, don't hesitate," Ruth's friend said almost cheerfully. "I can handle both of you."

The scourges glared at me, but remained still. Ruth's friend gestured me to walk down the steps first. I did it, feeling as if the Thorsens were pushing thumbtacks into me.

Along the way I asked, "Why are you doing so much to help me? Those guys are fiends."

"They're nothing," my new chum said confidently. "As for why I'm doing it, it's because you're Ruth's brother."

I had found out his name by the next block. He was Chet Glassford. My father had a married couple with that name as prescription customers and Chet told me that they were his uncle and aunt, who he visited every so often, and that he'd been raised in my town.

He suddenly looked to one side, alert. "We're not going in the right direction for your dad's store."

"I'm bringing some books back to the library."

"River Walk annex, sure. I remember it." He shrugged lightly. "I was never what you'd call comfortable over there."

All the same, he led the way correctly to the place.

After that, he suggested that we use Kleck's Pool, the local name for a rock-bordered section of the river where kids went swimming in the nude. I said regretfully that I had to go home and help in the store before getting down to my night's homework. Chet walked with me.

Chet, as he told me to call him and which I did, feeling very grown-up, was the family's guest for supper. The store had been closed and we were in our living quarters above. It was one of mom's routine meals, except for the hot chocolate pudding with cream stirred from the top of a milk bottle.

Dad turned to our guest once the coffee was finished. "Ruth insisted I follow your suggestion and see Zander Thorsen about the trouble his boys are giving Alva."

"You sound as if you're sorry you did it, sir."

Dad shrugged. "Zander knows his boys play rough, sometimes, but he's sure they wouldn't set out to hurt anybody unless they'd been provoked."

Mom put in, "I'd like to tell them a few home truths, him and Min Thorsen both."

"Don't do that," dad said, worried about further annoying a customer of the store's. "Let me tell you what happened next. Zander and Min called those boys in and asked if they'd swear that they hadn't tried to seriously harm Alva. Min said staunchly that her boys don't lie, and they said they'd do it. Zander then hauled out the family Bible and they swore, each with a hand on the Good Book."

Ruth, who had been dutifully helping mom gather up the dishes, asked, unbelievingly, And you just left after that?"

"I'd taken up enough of their time," dad said. "Tomorrow morning, though, Bible or not, I suppose I ought to take you to school and pick you up afterwards, boy."

I didn't expect anything to work out smoothly, and of course it didn't. When I came down to the store earlier than usual, next morning, the back pants pocket in which dad kept his car keys was empty. He was in his white professional jacket and smooshing around some ointment with his spatula. "Dave Osreicher needs this for his youngest, and I promised I'd have it for him ASAP." He looked at me wihout being at all apologetic." Mom has just gone to Roerum's Drug so she can obtain some neosynephrine for another prescription, and Ruth took the car for a delivery at the Westons."

I thought of asking Chet Glassford to help, but there almost certainly wasn't enough time for him to come and walk shotgun for me.

"Anybody you could walk with?" dad asked.

There was, but my friends would vanish at the first sight of the terrible two.

"Well, be careful, then," dad said, and turned away.

"I'll be okay," I said, trying to sound like Popeye the Sailor Man.

I didn't bring a pocket knife, certain that one of the scourges would boot it out of my hand if they started at me again and I went after it. The only precautions I could take were to perch my glasses in a side pocket of my pants and look around to my back and sides as usual. This time the closed stores and sun-touched houses I passed looked fuzzy, and more than one customer was first to say hello to me for once. A few of them, amused, asked what I'd done with my glasses and I guess I made some weak little joke out of the temporary nudity.

My troubles didn't get under way till I was near the school premises. Elroy heaved into sight first, his girth blocking out a chunk of the May sun. He called out and hurried after me.

I had given some previous thought to what I'd do if the two-man gang tried to beat me up again and as a result I stood poised till Elroy was about three feet off and then kicked him hard. Elroy doubled up, cursing.

Omar had come at me from the north side and I had to turn. One-for-one made for rotten odds, especially against a Mack truck like Omar Thorsen.

"Here's where you get it, best student," he said, just as Elroy stumbled around back of me to hold my arms from behind. A few voices called out, protesting, but no witness came closer.

Omar looked me up and down contemptuously, and reached into that pocket of mine holding the substitute glasses, then knocked them to the ground and jumped on them in their case. The sound of breaking glass was so clear it seemed to leave an echo that grated on the eardrums.

And then Omar began to do the one thing I dreaded worst of all. He raised the frankfurter-sized second finger of his right hand and pushed it forcefully toward my right eye.

I shut both eyes tightly and moved my head to duck. It couldn't possibly have worked as well as it seemed to as there wasn't much space for me, but I felt no pain. Instead a howl proceeded from Omar Thorsen and another from Elroy just before my arms were freed.

A little fearfully, because I couldn't be sure something else might not have happened, I looked up to see Chet Glassford with two hard hands raised in karate chop style. He was looking triumphant.

There was good reason for his elation. The Thorsens offered no further resistance. The fight had been chopped out of them.

Omar, gray-faced, whispered to his brother, "Get moving, dummy! Out!"

He drew back before Elroy did and spoke to Chet with some difficulty, "We'll get him and you, too."

Chet Glassford, at perfect ease and with a smile that kept joviality at a distance, said, "Come around anytime, kids." His steely tone made the last word sound like the gravest insult. All of which made him the bravest man I'd ever met.

He didn't turn to me again until the Thorsens had moved out of earshot. "Ruth called me to say that your dad couldn't bring you over and asked if I would do it. I wasn't able to reach you before this."

"I'm awful glad you did reach me."

Of course I was admiring and grateful as he'd practically been a guardian angel to me, but I wasn't actually sure how I really felt. Face it, Chet was only a visitor to River Walk and I'd be living here for a long time with my head practically sticking through the painted canvas to offer those Thorsens a sure target any time their mean streaks got the better of them.

What I said, tactfully—thinking all the time—was,

"They'll come after you, now."

Chet threw his head back and laughed genuinely this time. Let 'em try, and see how far they get with a grown-up."

No doubt he looked forward to their trying to take him by surprise, with Elroy failing to hold both arms behind Chet while Omar couldn't take one of his eyes out.

And just for a passing minute, I don't mind saying I felt a little sorry for Elroy and even for Omar.

My recollection is that on the next night I gave another demonstration of watching the television in action while getting my homework done effectively at the same time. Mom drifted into the parlor to glance at me, a bit startled, even though she knew I could it, and making mental notes to tell dad that the miracle was happening again. Dad didn't take the time to look in.

Just before eleven o'clock, the bedtime that had been decreed for me even though I was going on fifteen years of age, I finally closed the notebook, which I'd actually been finished with for the last forty minutes, and trudged upstairs.

A car was parking raggedly almost in front of the house. Deeply interested, I looked out my window. What kind of car it was has slipped my memory, but I did see a happy and hoydenish-looking Ruth climb out of it. Then she turned around, leaned toward the driver and planted a feathery kiss on one of Chet's paper-thin cheeks.

I would have heard the finish of the ball game on my

room radio if I had put it on quietly or been interested enough. The Cincinnati Reds were already far ahead. I don't see any point in drawing out an event where the finish is already known.

I was distracted on my way back from the washroom to hear mom and dad in the parlor, and Ruth's voice raised by way of response. I leaned over the stairwell to hear what sort of family problem had involved dad.

"He's not the sort of young man a girl like you should marry," mom said, her voice rising almost musically to counter Ruth's shrillness. "He's been a big help to Alva, agreed, he's been very pleasant. True, he's connected to people we've known our whole lives long, but nobody really knows what he's been doing in the last few years. Your father agrees with me."

Dad made the humming sound I'd heard before, as if he was interested but not really part of the conversation. I'd been wrong to think of him as a full participant.

"I'll tell you something you don't know, mom. If I encourage Chet, he'll settle up his business affairs in Denver and come back to River Walk and marry me."

Mom must have turned angrily on dad. "Why don't you say something? You're part of this family, too."

And dad spoke quietly, using words I'd heard from him any number ot times before. "It's not the time to do anything about this."

And mom, bitterly, "For you, it's *almost* never the time."

That *almost* of hers was rich. I couldn't think when

dad had considered it was ever time to do something for a family member.

The squabbling sounded like it would go on until dawn. If I kept listening I'd end up too tired to appreciate the biology experiments the next morning at school.

I turned away from the noise just as mom was saying, "Your father told me he feels the way I do," and scooted back to my room.

A quick last-minute check with the radio showed that the Reds had hit eight homers since I stopped watching, and had just loaded the bases. I turned off my radio for the night and closed my eyes, ready for sleep.

My eyes didn't stay closed for long.

A scream came to my ears, the sound of some male experiencing terror. I raced to the window. Lights were coming on. Dad, who must've gone out for a walk to get away from the female argument, came running to the house. He didn't ask if we were safe, though. Over the sound of sobbing, I saw dad call to a neighbor, offering to phone the police right away. Mr. Clitheroe, the neighbor, thanked dad and promised to do that much himself. I closed a window and went to bed, deciding I'd wait till the police came. I did stay awake for a few more minutes.

My last thought was to realize that Chet's car was gone and I was glad he wouldn't get in any trouble. Chet was a friend, after all, as well as the only guardian angel I had.

Next morning I asked Ruth if she'd call Chet to come over and escort me to school. Sadly, she told me that Chet had left town late last night.

I was still quaking inside when I realized that dad had given in to mom's urging to take me to school. "I never thought those boys would try it again," he added, referring to last night's troubles and making me sick at the thought that had crossed my mind. Not Chet! They wouldn't be able to harm Chet!

Dad's car was getting its six-month overhaul and he never thought of making my morning easier by driving mom's car instead. We walked.

Neither Thorsen was in sight, which suited me very nicely, thank you. Dad, stopping finally to talk with some of his friends about last night, didn't notice me going to the nearly spotless schoolyard. Nobody I ran into knew what had happened.

The Thorsens were still nowhere to be seen. By the time I was inside the building, I felt like it was just another day.

At attendance, where we checked in every weekday morning, Mr. Kanarek saw me looking mystified and grateful at the empty seats usually occupied by the Brothers Thorsen.

"I have to tell you all," he said, in the booming voice that could have wilted flowers, "that one of our students has been hospitalized at River Walk General on Allerton Street. I'm referring to Omar Thorsen."

There was a startled murmur from almost everybody but me. Chet seemed to have given Omar Thorsen a terrible time when the brothers tried ganging up on him, I was sure. My only regret was that Omar would eventually get out of the hospital.

"I want the first student in each row to walk that row with one of these plastic glasses and collect twenty-five cents from each of you so that whenever visitors are eventually allowed, we can send or bring a suitable gift for poor Omar."

I heard money clicking against plastic interiors. Violet Jardine, the strong-willed girl who was a full three years older than me, nodded approvingly when she saw that I hadn't kicked in.

I had to stand up afterwards and tell Mr. Kanarek in front of the whole class that I refused to help cheer up the afflicted Omar. Mr. Kanarek talked about returning good for evil, but made no headway.

The week raced on. Elroy came back to school, which made me tighten up for a while, but he only looked expressionlessly at me when I came across him. I suppose he was waiting for a revitalized Omar to join him in pounding on me, but now he didn't talk. Not to me or anybody else.

Three more weeks surged by before Violet Jardine sat down next to me in study hall and whispered, "Omar Thorsen is coming back tomorrow. Somebody told me it's definite."

I tightened up a little on the inside.

Violet, who wouldn't have stood patiently for trouble from anybody, suggested, "You ought to carry a pocket knife now, and show it around. Guys like Omar and

Elroy don't want to take a chance something might go wrong."

There was no point telling her that the Thorsens would probably take that knife first and make a few cuts in me with it.

Omar Thorsen, when I saw him on my way to biology class, narrowed his hot brown eyes for seconds, then looked away without word one. I'd be surprised if I didn't turn pale, but nothing passed between us. I hurried away to be the first student inside, so I could talk to Mr. Besserer for a minute.

In class, Omar was asked to write something on the blackboard. As soon as he took the chalk in his right hand, I saw for the first time that there was a gap between his first and third fingers. The second finger, with which he'd apparently tried to take out one of my eyes, had been cut off.

I can still remember being distracted enough from a class problem, for once, to call out with shock.

"Nobody warned me what to expect, maybe because they didn't know themselves, but it's easy enough now to realize what happened," I said to the folks over a light June supper. "The Thorsens attacked Chet Glassford and he got the better of them. He cut off Omar's finger and warned both of the guys to leave me alone and tell nobody who'd done it to them or Elroy would lose a finger, too."

Ruth said quickly, "I'll write and tell him how grateful we all are for everything he did. Chet is a good man to have on our side."

Mom snapped to attention. "Not as part of our family by marriage he isn't. Your father agrees with me that Chet wouldn't be an asset in that way at all."

"But you must realize that Chet Glassford may have kept Alva from losing his health, his sight, even his life!" Ruth protested.

"Chet Glassford may not stop at using violence on a Thorsen, Ruthie, and your father thinks so, too," mom persisted. "Suppose you marry him and there's a bitter argument between you, which can certainly happen in the course of a marriage. If he gets mad enough, he might do something violent to you. The very possibility will scare you out of your mind and work against your long-term happiness."

An ache-filled silence passed before Ruth said, "I'll never write or talk to him again if you think I shouldn't."

"Yes, I do think so, and your dad feels the same way," mom said firmly. "Well treat Chester Glassford as a good friend if he ever comes back to River Walk. We'll help him like we'd help any neighbor. We'll never mention what happened and we don't let him get very friendly with any of us."

Dad was the one who punctuated that statement for my benefit, turning toward me. Our eyes met, and as soon as that happened he looked away. For a minute, though, just for a minute, he'd been interested in one member of his family.

There isn't much more to tell. Dad went back to behaving as if he was on coolly correct terms with his family. Ruthie married her on-again-off-again boyfriend Wally Porter, who makes a decent living for her and their kids. Chet came back for a visit when I was away galloping through the University of Michigan. He got married to the heartily aggressive Violet Jardine, the schoolmate I'd helped with science assignments. He moved her to Denver, where I understand she keeps him pretty much under control. As for the Thorsens, they grew a little older and moved out with their family to Las Vegas. Nobody in town ever heard from them again, as far as I know. A great loss to everybody, I'm sure.

I didn't get back to River Walk for even a week's stay till dad's final illness. My wife, who was pregnant, and our two kids missed Salt Lake City as much as I did, but computers had just come in and at least I was able to keep track of events in the office and get a lot of my work done.

Dad didn't talk to me much, as usual, but he did find time to give my oldest son his ring and to give the younger one a good luck token my grandfather had passed on to him. Every so often he looked at me as if he wanted to tell me something before he went to join mom, but when there was somebody else in his hospital room he wouldn't send that person away so we could be alone and when I did it he stared up at the ceiling, wordless.

Dad's lawyer gave me the small but heavy envelope just before the funeral, as he'd been instructed to do. It held the possession left to me by the man who had kept quiet about the major crisis of my younger years. He had used mom as a spokesperson to keep my sister from marrying a man who'd have been wrong for her in any circumstances. Not till I was holding what was inside that envelope, the undersized surgical knife like those I had seen as a student in High School biology class, not till then did the best student at Westside High finally realize that Chet Glassford wouldn't have cared enough to perform that ghastly deed on my behalf. Only one man had cared enough to save my future.

I cried quietly through most of the funeral ceremony, crying for dad's inability to reach out to his family and my own failure to truly understand his feelings. More than one neighbor told me solemnly afterwards that no one ever realized how close I had truly been to my— my father.

DANGER! MAN BEHIND YOU!

Lake walked ahead purposefully, his cold eyes never leaving the man he followed. The man didn't know anybody followed; he walked along slowly and glanced in at store windows.

Lake's coat collar was pulled up around his ears, the tips almost cherry-red in the early morning cold. One hand in his pocket almost covered the shape of two sides of a square with an arc under its crotch.

This was a shopping district. Stores were shuttered, not yet opened for the day's business.

Lake nodded once to himself, then caught up with the man, gripped him around the neck and pulled him into a store vestibule.

"Sorry about this," Lake grunted. "Nothing personal."

He had said those words so many times in the past that he couldn't possibly have counted them.

The man's tongue seemed jammed between his teeth as he tried to send air through the semi-circle between tongue and upper teeth. They finally formed a syllable.

"Th...th—"

Lake took out the gun and fired. The man's knobby hands clenched over his stomach and he fell up against the window glass. He slid down easily at first, then with a sudden thump. The tip of his tongue showed between rows of dingy teeth.

Lake glanced out at the street before bending over the body, a hand to the heart. With a half-nod he straightened, then stood very still a second.

A flick of movement had caught his attention. He looked around quickly, the gun up.

Inside the store, a man hesitated over the opened register. An upended bag, from which silver coins streamed into the machine, shook in his hands. He was small and thin with blond hair that looked dusty through the glass.

"Goddam!" Lake said softly.

He rattled the doorknob, then reversed the gun so that its butt was inches from the glass. After breaking a section of it, he reached through and around to unlock the door.

Inside, the little man scuttled past the customer counter and out of sight.

Lake ran into the back room, paused briefly with hands on hips. An exit door swung open on a city backyard. No one was in sight.

Lake scowled. The store sold books and magazines and the cheese-like smell of cloth-bound books bothered him. He walked out slowly, like a man on the way to work.

Down the block he turned into a candy store and

waited till the clerk gave him change in dimes and nickels. He had to go from one booth to the other because the first phone was out of order.

"Mr. Bundy?" he began, once he'd dialed the number and settled his coat around him. "That piece of business you assigned me to, it came out all right for the most part."

"What went wrong?" Bundy sounded almost bored. He never greeted people to whom he spoke on the phone.

"I might have to make a trip for a few weeks—maybe even months."

"No," Bundy said firmly. "You're a good man and I don't want to lose you."

"Maybe there won't be any choice."

"If anything's in the way, get it out of the way. Anything or anybody. Am I clear?"

Lake nodded uselessly, then said, "Sure." He wasn't at all jarred by the notion of what would be involved.

"I'll need information, to start out with."

"Well?"

Lake eyed the holes of the disc as he talked. "I have to know about the owner of a store called Bookville on 118 Clove Street. That's one-one-eight Charlie-Louis-Oscar-Victor-Edward. Clove Street. The store's a hole-in-the-wall operation, maybe only one guy working it. If I'm wrong and there are clerks, I need their names and addresses. I need descriptions of everybody."

He waited till the sound of Bundy's pencil scratching finally stopped; the man's memory was notoriously bad.

"And it might be a help to know," he added, "if anybody there asked for police protection this morning."

"Don't think I can get the last for you," Bundy said carefully. "How fast do you need this stuff?"

"Ten-fifteen minutes at the outside. I have to get moving."

"That's impossible, but call back, anyhow."

Lake stayed in the booth. He lit a cigarillo, clicked on the booth fan and waited. Patience was one of his strong points. Every so often he opened the door a few inches to let out smoke-clouds.

Promptly fifteen minutes later, he phoned back.

"Lucky break for you," Bundy said by way of greeting. "One of the clerks in the county courthouse looked up the business name. Owner is Roy Niden. That's Nathan, Ida Dennis, Edward, Nathan—Niden. His home address is 1841 Lantern Road." Bundy spelled out the location. "He's a short guy with blond hair. The store's a one-man operation, like you thought."

"How do you know that?"

"Told you you'd been lucky." Bundy's chuckle was a dry, unnerving series of noises. "Clerk happens to know the guy personally. Says that Niden's one of those very hard workers, very conscientious guy, if that's any help."

It explained why the man had been in the store so early in the morning, before opening time.

"Says the guy can't make really important decisions on his own. Has to talk 'em over with somebody. Is that any help?"

"Maybe." Roy Niden would have to make up his mind about going to the police—maybe. Lake punched a hand against the wall of the booth. "Who does he usually talk 'em over with?"

"Girlfriend, name of Katherine Ames. Hard-shell cookie, the brains of the combo. They figure to get married."

Lake pursed his lips. "Any address for her?"

"Try the phone book," Bundy said dryly. He chuckled. If the girl's nothing to look at, all you got to do is put a flag over her face and...."

Lake laughed dutifully. He disliked smut, always had.

On the bus, he waited with folded hands, looking out at the streets. When the bus conductor stopped to argue with a truck driver, Lake sighed and picked up a newspaper from the next seat.

He left the bus some two blocks from the building in which Katherine Ames lived. On the way, because of an impulse, he stepped into another booth to buzz Roy Niden's home phone number. The dime was returned so forcefully it fell to the floor; he let it lie there.

Katherine Ames lived in a rundown tenement. Under the typewritten name on the downstairs doorbell sloth, the apartment number had been engraved. He walked up, a hand extending one pocket so that the gun-shape wouldn't be clearly seen.

It occurred to him that she and Niden might not be there, or might be living with people who would see him when he appeared. He shrugged it off.

From behind the apartment door, a girl called out cautiously, "Who is it?"

"Miss Ames? Want to talk with you."

He pulled down the flaps of his coat and brushed back his dark hair with a hand. The door opened slowly, squeaking.

"I was expecting somebody else," Katherine Ames said pleasantly, wiping her long fingers on a red-and-white checkered apron. Obviously she's been preparing food. She ws a small blonde, coming up to Lake's shoulder.

"Do you live here alone, Miss Ames?"

"It just happens that I do." Lake didn't show any relief.

"Were you expecting Roy Niden? Or is he here, already?"

"I don't think that's any of your business," the girl said coolly, putting on a pair of shell-rimmed glasses. "Whatever *you're* selling, I can't use any."

Lake's foot was solidly in the door. "I'm sorry to have to tell you this, but Niden's wanted."

"By whom?"

Lake shrugged, then gave a thin smile.

"You're a policeman?"

He took out a wallet and allowed her a fleeting glimpse of a toy badge that he'd often used to good effect.

"I don't believe it," she said decisively. "Anybody else maybe, but not Roy. A mistake somewhere."

"Just as you like, Miss." Politeness came easily to him. "Probably a mix-up we can straighten out after Mr. Niden takes a short trip downtown. I'd like to wait here for him, Miss, if you don't mind."

Bleak wintry sunshine was reflected in the girl's eyeglasses, so that for a little while she didn't seem to have any eyes at all, just a chunk of cloud between the shell rims.

"Suit yourself," she said finally. "Roy should have been here by now. He sounded excited just a little while ago, over the phone."

"Maybe he's so scared he can't move fast," Lake shrugged. "I've seen it happen. Does he come up to see you often, in the mornings?"

"Never done it before."

Lake, sitting down, finally let out a long pent-up sigh.

The girl asked calmly, "What station do you work out of?"

He didn't hesitate more than a second. "Twenty-fifth precinct."

"Your name?"

"Hughes. Oliver Hughes."

Kit Ames turned swiftly. Lake heard the buzz of a telephone dial tone.

He rose in a single hard movement and gripped her neck in the crook of his arm. Kit Ames screamed once, then tried to kick. Her blows connected under one kneecap. Lake extended the reach of one hand already over her mouth, till it covered her nostrils as well.

Kit Ames flapped briefly with her arms, kicked out and then was still.

Lake could hear his watch ticking before he took away his hands. Kit Ames would have dropped to the floor, but he softened it and lifted the girl in his arms. He dropped her hard on a sofa.

Outside but nearby, a window opened up and woman called out, "Did you hear somebody scream?"

"Yeah, a woman. Don't ask me who. I dunno."

Two women leaning out their windows and exchanging gossip. Their voices floated upward in the cold morning air.

"Do you think we ought to call a policeman?"

"Nah. Besides, whenever you want on eyou can't find him. He's out chasing pushcart peddlers or taking graft." The woman added brightly. "Tell me, what are you cooking for dinner, tonight?"

Lake looked down at Katherine Ames. Briefly he felt for a pulse, then nodded; one part of the day's work was done.

A hissing sound from the kitchen took Lake there. Coffee was perking. To Lake the familiar sound was one of the best inducements to get a man out of bed in the morning.

Lake finally put on gloves, and poured himself a cup of coffee. He discovered milk in the refrigerator and doughnuts in the small white cupboard next to the kitchen table.

One of the nearby windows on a lower floor opened noisily and the woman who'd wanted to call the police was talking.

"That woman who yelled before, she stopped it now."

"That's funny, come to think of it," the other one answered. "After a yowl like that, you'd think she'd cry to beat the band. Just quiet, though. Too quiet, if y'ask me."

"Now do you think we ought to call the police?"

"I hate to get mixed up with anything. I always mind my own business. But this time, I guess we can't help it."

A window was closed abruptly.

Lake shrugged. Making sure that he couldn't be seen through any of the windows, he washed the coffee cup and saucer and put back in place. He did it quickly with an eye on the big electric clock above the cupboard and an ear cocked for sounds.

Kit Ames' keys hung from a kitchen nail. He took them and closed the door from the outside. A dab of sweat sprinkled his forehead on the way down, but only in the change of climate. His steps were slow, deliberate.

In order to prolong his time in the neighborhood, Lake stepped into the corner grocery directly across the street. From there, as he waited his turn to be served, he had a good view of the street entrance to the apartment building in which Kit Ames had lived.

A police car reached the curb eventually, and two cops in uniform stepped out and disappeared into the building.

Lake ordered a bottle of milk from the grocer, then

stepped out to the street. Casually looking back, as if out of curiosity and nothing more, he walked down the street.

Two blocks away, he stepped into another tenement and left the milk in front of a doorstep. He held Katherine Ames' keys till he found a manhole, then dropped them and stirred them in with a foot.

In a bar he made another phone call. It was a policy of Bundy's that, if possible, Lake had to report every two hours.

"Things are coming along," he said vaguely.

"Our friend hasn't shown up at the store yet," Bundy said, referring to Niden of course. "By the way, there's a message for you. Some broad called and passed it to my secretary."

"What?"

"Message is not to forget the saccharine. What the hell!"

"It's personal," Lake smiled lightly. "Thanks."

Over a beer, he frowned at the barkeep, who was making notations on what was probably a racing form. Before he was finished drinking, Lake suddenly snapped his fingers, wiped off the foam mustache with the back of a gloved hand and stepped outside for a cab.

Lake hated cabs. He would always write down amounts of fares in a little ten-cent notebook he kept for listing expenses; but he rode tight-lipped, leaning forward on a comfortable seat and tightly gripping the silken rope back of the driver's seat.

He found no difficulty getting into Roy Niden's apartment, thanks to a skeleton key, and no problem getting out. When he left he was grim; Niden hadn't been there in hours.

In his anger, hands behind his back as he walked, he passed Matterhorn Avenue, following the line of tree-shaded apartment houses till it brought him down to Clove Street.

In his preoccupation he was nearly run over as he crossed Daniel Webster Park, a triangular block with a statue of Webster in the center. He glared at a large sign in front of a movie theater advertising, *"Big Horror and Fun Show for kids from 6 to 60—Come In and Forget Your Troubles."*

Bookville was closed. Gaps still showed in the door glass where Lake had smashed it in. Calmly, almost sedately, Lake walked around the corner and slipped into the store by the back entrance. Niden had been there in the morning, at a time when the place was apparently closed.

Lake was satisfied that the story was empty when he heard talk in the vestibule. Looking out briefly, he saw a policeman talking to Roy Niden, their breaths coating the glass set into the door panel.

The lock snapped open. As soon as the door opened as well, the automatic burglar alarm started to keen on the nerves like a dentist's drill. Niden scurried to a space at the right of his lending library racks and turned it off.

"So far, so good," he said.

"You got nothin' to worry about, now," the cop told him breezily. "What more could you want than protection? Glad you finally made up your mind the right way."

"If not for Katherine, what happened to her...."

The words had fallen into a deep pool of silence. Niden squared his shoulders as he walked.

The first shot dropped him, the second hit his falling body. The third shot took care of the cop. Lake waited, looking out to see if there was any further movement. When he walked out to the front, he stooped over briefly. The cop was dead. A thread of pulse wound itself through Niden's body; another shot finished him.

Lake went out the back way. On the street he took a cab. He reported to Bundy in person, then stopped into a drugstore for a bottle of saccharine; and finally took his car out of the parking lot.

As he drove he relaxed, his breath coming easier and slower. He whistled for a while, then, reminded, turned on the radio and let himself relax on the road.

He didn't stop the car till he reached the suburbs and a small house where a tall woman smiled at him from the porch, then waved and turned back into the house. When Lake had parked in the garage, he turned to see his small son advancing on him.

"Dad-ee...!"

Over dinner, Mrs. Lake said, "I'm glad you brought the saccharine, dear. Now tell me, how'd the day's work go?"

"Like a day's work usually does." He shrugged. "the

job's gotta be done, though, and that's it."

Mrs. Lake touched his hands with hers. "I'm sure you're good at it."

"With a wife and kid to support a guy has to work hard," he smiled expansively. "It ain't every job that could pay a mug like me enough o live in a section like this and have his own house and all."

She looked down at the boy. "He won't have to go into your business."

"Not him, he's gonna be smart." Lake smiled. "There's gotta be an easier way to make a buck."

RING IN THE NEW

"Would you hire that man, dear?" Joyce asked. "That man over there?"

"I wouldn't *have hired* him in my worst hour."

He had made a point of gently correcting his wife's grammar because he wanted to be accurate. These days he wasn't in a position to hire or fire or make any business decisions at all, and he was damned glad of it. Glad to be taking it easy with Joyce on "A" deck of the *S.S. Caribbean Majesty*, flanked by other passengers in gravel-colored deck chairs all waiting lazily for the first lunch offering.

"But that guy does stick out too much," Neal added, glancing at the ugly seaman with the thrust-out jaw and rough skin that would always need shaving. Neal was barely able to talk over the sound of ping-pong rackets crashing repeatedly into a ball further along the deck. "I tested and hired only ordinary-looking guards to be sent out uniformed by the Peacock Agency. None of them were a bit like that joker."

True enough. The seaman had been cursed with a liver-colored complexion, a frankfurter-sized neck, yam-shaped eyes and that chin flat as a pancake, altogether like an indigestible meal. The man was turning his head again and again as he moved, probably searching for one particular person. When he stopped himself, his lips thinned in a smile.

The girl who had come on deck, youngest among the seated retired males and their preening wives, was a fragile-looking blonde with the slimmest of figures and most of her shapely legs almost hidden by a white-striped blue skirt.

The seaman didn't seem to care that she flinched at the sight of him, his smile widening as he hurried toward her. The blonde turned left, making sure that somebody else, anybody else, was in sight.

Almost automatically, Neal poised himself to get between seaman and blonde, unaware that Joyce had been holding one of his not-yet-suntanned arms while applying only the lightest pressure to keep him in place.

He would have gone further if the blonde hadn't turned away and hurried inside, losing herself in the growing crowd. Probably she hadn't seen or noticed Neal.

"I'll bet everything I know about people that that girl will be the cause of trouble," Neal said.

Joyce knew her husband's skills as a judge of people's potential for disturbing the peace. She didn't argue.

Neal saw the ugly seaman and the fragile blonde for the second time in the evening when he and Joy were making their way along the lounge on "B" deck to attend the captain's welcoming cocktail party. He was distracted at first by a man's voice speaking urgently.

Some twenty yards down the spotless passage, that memorably ugly seaman stood glowering down at the fragile young blonde. Bitterness was in his posture as well as his voice and the crooked smile that reflected no enjoyment whatever.

Neal took a tense breath, causing Joyce to glance along the hall in turn and whisper to him, "Don't get into it."

"Not even to help a sure loser, otherwise?" he asked quietly.

As they paused, the blonde started to turn away.

The ugly seaman said in a husky tone, "You never in weeks and weeks would give me any chance."

The girl looked behind her for help, nodded gratefully at the sight of Neal, and only then did she start to move away. The seaman, not having seen an intruder, reached out to grip one of her shoulders. He was suddenly stopped by Neal deftly interposing himself between him and the girl.

The seaman's pinched eyes met Neal's. Muttering to himself as the girl hurried off, he walked slowly to the nearest staircase, scowled back, then started down....

* * * * * * *

"...All right this time, but from now on let's mind our own business," his wife said when Neal rejoined her, showing the sternness of an ex-High School teacher, her vocation when they met and got married.

Neal had every intention of reporting the incident to Captain Robert Eiken, now shaking hands affably with all comers. The captain excused himself just before it was Joyce's turn to be greeted, and the handsome executive officer took the duty, smiling mechanically at all.

With a glass of dry white wine in hand, Neal was starting back to talk with the captain when the girl he had helped approached, smiling. She was the sort of sharp-nosed and thin-lipped girl that young fellows of Neal's generation had said must be sexually frigid, but this one's usually merry and appreciative eyes told the opposite story. Neal believed the windows of the soul instead of verbal graffiti. He himself had developed a mild case of glaucoma in one eye, most likely provoked by his equally mild diabetes, but he could still depend on eyesight as well as common sense.

"Thank you very much for the favor," she said in a voice soft and musical. "I think that Floyd will be convinced now that I don't want anything to do with him."

"Oh, you know the man."

"Floyd Blackhouse introduced himself to me during one of the orientation sessions. When I say 'introduced'—"

"Then you work on board?"

"Surely. That's why I wear sky-blue with a white stripe, the shipping line's colors. I'm in one boutique or another, depending on who's short of staff that particular day."

"Which also means that Floyd what's-his-face can keep track of you."

"He won't be a bother after that run-in with you, Mr.—I didn't hear your name."

"Neal. Neal Westland. This is my wife, Joyce."

The executive officer, second-in-command on board, a darkly handsome man, appeared and introduced himself to the Westlands as Perry Hartrig. Hardly had they responded when he was turning anxiously to the girl.

"You're looking upset, Gail. What's wrong?"

Before she could say anything, another officer on the dais announced a postponement of the next show in the night club, then called Hartrig's name and rank.

Joyce looked thoughtfully after the young exec's receding back. "He wears a big chunky ring, doesn't he?"

Gail, the young woman, smiled. "He took my word about its use in fighting off female passengers, and bought it at one of the shops. That was the first time I ever talked to him."

The usually observant Neal, who hadn't noticed the ring, told himself awkwardly that Gail could probably talk a man into buying anything....

Back at their cabin on "B" deck, after a tasty filling dinner, Neal and Joyce found two apples and a banana on the cocktail table, probably to keep them from starving to death between the ample dinner and one of those magnificent midnight buffets. Neal laughed so hard at that notion he came close to forgetting altogether about Floyd-whosis and the fragile blonde named Gail.

He spoke to her again the next morning at the five o'clock pre-breakfast of clear soup with crackers, coffee and toasted Danish. Joyce had decided to wait in their cabin for the daily one-page ship's bulletin of late world news.

Gail Abbott gave her full name as she sat gracefully next to him on "C" deck aft, and was talking about the Floyd-whosis problem before he brought it up.

"You won't have to worry about me for the rest of the trip, Mr. Westland."

"Being on a cruise makes everybody an optimist," Neal remarked blandly. "How can you be sure you won't have any more trouble from Floyd—uh, Blackhouse?"

"I've managed to catch the eye of Perry Hartrig, the Executive Officer, and we'll be seen around together so often that Floyd will know he's sure to catch hell from a superior if he goes near me again. For all I can tell you, he may have seen me and Perry on deck last night."

And she smiled Eve's smile, the one that every woman may learn in the womb itself, the smile of a female anchored in youth that would never fade, in a beauty that couldn't leave.

Back at the cabin, he ran an eye over the sports news and stock quotes on the ship's bulletin sheet, then took Joyce in to breakfast. He must have been the two-hundredth passenger that morning who said he'd weigh a ton by trip's end. Not that it mattered any more, except for his health. He didn't have to go in and work at the Peacock Protection Agency and toe the line, thank heavens.

Joyce waited until early afternoon just before the first lifeboat drill of the cruise, then chuckled familiarly and reached an arm around his midriff while loosening his belt with the other hand.

"Want to go out, handsome?" she drawled from one side of her mouth. "Bet I'm the easiest pickup you ever had."

"We've only got twenty minutes before the drill starts."

"Better hurry, handsome...."

They were grinning afterwards, a married couple who knew each other's heartbeats and knew everything else about each other.

Neither had budgeted extra time to put on life jackets, so it seemed to Neal during the last minutes that no appearance at the lifeboat drill would be put in by at least one couple. He was feeling too placed to care, but no signal had sounded so he might as well give it his best try.

He happened to be finished and tying the front of Joyce's life jacket, which she seemed to think disparagingly ought to have been a designer original "at these cruise prices," when the drill summons wailed at last.

They hurried down to their station at the fore part of "C" deck in sight of the outdoor swimming pool, now deserted. An older couple Neal had been avoiding was there first and he listened expressionlessly to the man talking about how important it was for "us retired old crocks" to have hobbies. It turned out during the course of the talk that each couple had one divorced son. It was possible to have too much in common with others.

Gail Abbott joined the passengers. Inexplicably she was smiling, a hundred percent at ease. Didn't she realize that her presence at a drill might attract an unwelcome admirer, making her and everybody else miserably angry?

Moments passed before Neal became aware that it wasn't likely to make the least difference, knowledge which followed a sound of throat-clearing as some-body signaled for their attention.

"Good afternoon, ladies and gentlemen," said Perry Hartrig, raising his voice to make himself heard by those passengers joining the others. "I am the Executive Officer and we're going to rehearse what to do in case of need."

Calling Gail to the center of the group, where she joined him, he demonstrated how a life jacket should be put on, and she showed how to ease the way into the lifeboat. He was attentive and courteous to all, but he had eyes only for the delicious-looking Gail Abbott.

It was Neal who first saw the seaman at the fringe of this group. The ugly Blackhouse, his weak-tea eyes narrowed, was opening and closing his fists as he stared at the only beautiful girl on board. He must have known better than to go near Gail Abbott from now on, but Neal, watching, didn't think, somehow, that the hard times for Gail were over.

Most passengers rushed to shore at the first cruise

stop early the next morning. What with the sleepy pleasures of La Guaira, with soft calypso music almost everywhere they went, with buildings the same color as melting butterscotch, and a chance to buy duty-free merchandise, which Joyce certainly took advantage of, Neal didn't see Blackhouse or Gail again until evening on board.

He found Gail after dinner. Joyce had belatedly gone down to the purser's square to salt away the credit cards she had insisted on taking, and he walked the deck to help his so-called dietetic dinner settle into new quarters. The chilly *gazpacho* was getting along just fine with the spice-tinged *lamchi* and *boonchi*, he decided, when he heard Gail's unmistakable rippling laughter. Under the bright circular lights aft on "B" deck, she was playing a vigorous game of shuffleboard with the attentive Perry Hartrig.

When the exec unwillingly excused himself, saying, "It's my job to inspect the whole ship at about this time, you know, and see things are all right. I'd better make a pass at it, finally."

She was the first to notice Neal's proximity, but Hartrig made up for the distraction caused by Gail's very presence, and asked for almost a minute-to-minute rundown of Neal and Joyce's day. After being assured for the second time that the Westlands were enjoying everything on board, he left to do the job for which he was being paid.

Alone with Gail and certain that the exec was out of earshot, Neal said, "That man, Blackhouse, is still brooding about you."

"I've had better men than Floyd Blackhouse brooding about me," Gail answered, cheerful now that any possible awkwardness seemed a thing of the past.

Neal asked, "Then you still don't think he'll act up again?"

"Of course everything is all right. I'll go off by myself right now and there'll be no trouble. I hope to see you and your wife at the Midnight Tropical Fiesta later on."

She started off. Neal, looking after that perfect figure and thinking that she was amused by his being drawn uselessly to her, winced when she was out of his sight. He stayed in place, ears cocked, ready to jump up. Eventually he released a deep breath.

She was no part of his generation or his life. Besides, he was happily retired now, distanced by the world from its messes and trying to make believe he still carried responsibilities on his shoulders.

A waste of time, a waste of feelings.

He still felt hung over without the headache when he stopped off at the cabin to take a prescribed single drop of his glaucoma medicine. That done, he started to "A" deck to look for Joyce and found her on the other side of the sliding-glass doors at the shiny wooden railing, where she looked like the dominant figure in some pseudo-artistic painting.

"It's so quiet," she said softly, taking his hand as she looked out at the green gelatin-like waters of the Caribbean. "So quiet, so beautiful, and nobody else on this deck knows that the loveliest sight in the world is right here."

"The sea is the second prettiest," he insisted, touching his wife's graying hair with a gentle forefinger. "Would you like to spend a little time in the cabin before hitting the movie and the night club?"

"Yes, that would be...nice, dear."

* * * * * * *

Gail Abbott hurried over to him on the sunny "A" deck in the early afternoon. Joyce happened to be explaining to him that the only way to win the ship's betting pool determining its speed on a given day was to bet either a high-field number or a low-field one. In their family, it was Joyce who had an affinity for numbers, taking care of bank business, paying bills, and she had even mastered the computer program used to file their income tax. Neal's only competence with figures showed in his use of a pocket-sized solar-powered adding machine.

Gail smiled edgily at him, reminding Neal, against his will, of the only woman with whom he'd had an extramarital affair, a short-term series of episodes coming right after what turned out to be their first son's temporary marriage.

"Have you seen Perry today?"

"Hartrig? There's no reason why I should have."

"We were supposed to take lunch together, but he didn't show up."

"Maybe there's some emergency keeping him away."

Neal didn't know whether scaring her at this point would be justified. "Ask one of the other officers."

"I did, and I haven't been told anything yet."

"Keep in touch with whomever you asked."

"Yes. Sure." She was going to say something more, but looked at Joyce and turned to walk along the sun-splotched deck and return to her day's work.

Joyce had become absorbed in a sheet of figures while the talk went on. Now she looked up slowly in mute inquiry.

"That was nothing much," he said, and applied himself even more vigorously to the task of figuring out his wife's detailed explanation of betting odds.

* * * * * * *

The second lifeboat drill of the cruise took place that afternoon, interrupting a bingo game as well as a bout of poker that didn't seem to have stopped since the sailing, shuffleboard, and gym rituals of different types. Neal found himself with Joyce near the lifeboat assigned to them. While she talked to a shipboard acquaintance about her recent duty-free shopping, he was explaining to another acquaintance that he and Joyce had sold their suburban home in Katonah, New York, soon after their younger son moved out, and went into a Manhattan co-op just before the bottom dropped out of the co-op market.

"Good afternoon, ladies and gentlemen," a voice said clearly and methodically, a voice Neal remembered. "My name is Floyd Blackhouse, and I'm a seaman."

Neal looked to one side, where Gail Abbott was, a surprising warm smile on her lips. She smiled at nearly everybody, which was part of her job, of course, but seemed to be putting more feeling into a conversation with the graying and reserved Oliver Denton, a well-known real estate developer from Columbus, Ohio, who was apparently on the verge of being drawn out of his shell. Considering Gail's looks and presence, no one could have blamed the man.

Blackhouse glared at her, realizing that she was now trusting the good will of yet another important man on board, a man who could ruin Floyd Blackhouse if the seaman caused even an appearance of trouble.

"Mr. Hartrig, the Executive Officer, is indisposed," Blackhouse said, speaking with difficulty, proceeding with the drill while he glared at Denton and Gail.

"The crew is combing the ship for Perry Hartrig," said the ship's doctor when Neal ran him to earth in the library with its small dark shelves of new books and magazines and, behind the navy-blue curtains, a series of video games for younger passengers. Joyce, who took an interest in computer technology, had dropped a steward's jaw not long ago by asking if facilities for virtual reality were on board.

Before Neal could bark out, "Has Gail Abbott made a statement?" not caring that his ruffled-honcho manner would offend Dr. Gerber, a seaman hurried into the library. Under a healthy-looking tan, the man's face was pasty. His eyes bulged.

Gerber walked over to one side, where the seaman

joined him, whispering urgently. "God Almighty!" More quietly he added, "I'll stop at the office and bring my bag, just in case."

Instinct warned Neal to follow at a distance. He reached "C" deck in time to see Perry Hartrig on a stretcher about to be carried below. Hartrig's handsome features were dark, and it seemed to Neal that something else about the man was different, some surprising and unexpected change that may have been minor but the inability to identify it was galling. Before Neal could look more closely, the dead man was awkwardly carried out of sight.

Neal was deciding who to talk to about the little he knew when he found Joyce on "A" deck.

"I hope you aren't going to get mixed up in whatever is wrong on ship."

"The captain wouldn't let me, even if I wanted to."

"You want to," Joyce said shrewdly. "You love being retired, but part of you wants to see if you're still as good at clearing up messes as when you were on the job."

Which was when a steward approached carefully. "Mr. Westland? Beg pardon, sir, but the captain would like to see you in his office."

* * * * * * *

Captain Robert Eiken's office was a softly-lit room with the painting and thick carpet to be expected in the office of any CEO without allergies. Calm, restful, good for thinking.

But, at the moment, noisy. Like a hive of angry bees.

Gail Abbott was speaking accusingly to the seaman, Floyd Blackhouse, who shouted back.

Captain Eiken's voice cut like a knife. "Quiet, both of you! Now, of I send both of you down."

In the painful silence he turned to Neal, asking how much Neal knew of Miss Abbott's troubles on board, which she had just reported to him. Neal filled the captain in, then gave a description of his job when he'd been working. No protest was heard when he followed by asking how Perry Hartrig had died.

"A knife in the back," Dr. Gerber responded, his face still gray after close contact with death. "He was found in a dark storage room on 'C' deck. It happened almost certain between last night and dawn."

A recollection was gnawing at Neal. For some reason he was remember Joyce having said something, having pointed out something to him.

"The ring," he said suddenly. "Hartrig wore a ring. As a matter of fact, I missed the sight of it when I met the man, but my wife saw it and mentioned it to me. I must have looked for it automatically when I saw the body just to confirm what she'd said, and thanks to her having been so alert I saw the evidence that is sure to wrap up this case."

Gerber said defensively, "I was too busy examining the body to notice a ring."

"Of course you were, doctor. My point is that the ring had been moved up toward the second knuckle. Nobody would wear a ring in that position on account of the discomfort."

"And you're telling us what?" Dr. Gerber frowned.

"Either a criminal ordered Hartrig to hand it over and he couldn't get it off, or the criminal tried to pull it off after having committed the murder."

"And he was killed for a ring? A miserable ring?"

Floyd Blackhouse suddenly bellowed in protest, strongly insisting he hadn't been near the dead man. If he ever needed help, he swore he'd never want to get it through the likes of Perry Hartrig, who was to lousy to rot in hell.

Captain Eiken shut him up, more fiercely this time.

Neal wasn't surprised to see anxiety lines between Gail Abbott's freshly plucked brows suddenly drawn down.

"*I* wouldn't have tried to steal Perry's ring, either." She had noticed Neal's keen glance and pretended she had just made a mildly comic remark.

"Do you think you're still fooling me?" He had said once that she'd be the cause of trouble on board. How right he'd been!

The girl's voice hardened. "If you've got an accusation to make against me, talk directly."

Neal showed his contempt by turning pointedly to the captain. "She's very confident of her good looks and the effects of an apparently sunny nature to persuade most people around to her arguments. It shouldn't surprise you that she's managed to use everybody she wanted to use."

"Like Floyd Blackhouse, for instance?"

"She certainly knew him before the trip. I once over-heard him start to say to her, 'You never in weeks and weeks would give me any chance with you.' We can all guess what he meant."

Gail Abbott forced a smile. "Captain, I just know you'll tell him you don't believe any of this nonsense."

A man ignored her, perhaps for the first time. "In other words, Westland, she dropped Floyd Blackhouse, and I suppose she took up with Hartrig."

"At some time during an earlier trip, she and Hartrig exchanged rings and she talked him into keeping quiet about their close relationship, saying she wanted to make their work easier in dealing with susceptible older adult travelers." Neal glanced down at the third finger of Gail Abbott's left hand. "Hartrig may have been sure they'd eventually live together on land, and Blackhouse would no longer be allowed close enough to her to see her ring."

Gail Abbott asked mockingly, "Did I kill Perry because I wanted a dead lover?"

"No, you did it because you found out that a rich real estate developer, an older man, a widower, was on board. You wanted to marry Oliver Denton and live in style. Perry Hartrig could've tried to block your plans, even if poor Floyd was too dazed to try. Floyd Blackhouse would be a natural suspect for Perry Hartrig's murder, and the line would keep the dreary news as quiet as possible."

"How did she do it?" Captain Eiken asked.

"The little darlin' waited till she left me by the

shuffleboard court last night, and lured Hartrig into a dark storeroom. Instead of their having some fun, she stabbed him. Most likely she hurried out to throw the bloody knife overboard, then came back to get the ring, and couldn't."

Captain Eiken frowned. "Yes, what about that ring?"

"She must have thought that, like almost everything else in her life, taking it off would give her no trouble whatever. After some frantic minutes, she realized she didn't have the strength for it. (By the way, Blackhouse could have managed it easily.) She knew that she had no choice except to bluff it out, starting by bringing the case against Blackhouse to the fore in advance of others like myself coming to you, making it clear she was telling everything. Until just a few minutes ago, her plans were working out just the way they nearly always did."

"You haven't told us yet, Mr. Westland, why she needed that ring of Hartrig's."

"The inscription inside the band was very likely to cause her to lose Denton, if it became public after the murder. That ring looks a lot like the sort that some couples exchange. Gail Abbott's name would be on it along with the date—we can check if I'm right and make a computer check later on among city records— the date on which she became Perry Hartrig's wife."

* * * * * * *

A relaxed and liberally tanned Neal didn't see Captain Eiken again until just before leaving the ship with Joyce.

"I've had an idea that you might want to offer to your company," Neal began. "The only problem on this trip could've been avoided if your crew and staff were checked out at work, where a trained observer could see how they relate to their jobs and to others, an observer who knows enough to be inconspicuous but can draw conclusions about them, and about passengers, too."

"Are you suggesting yourself for a job like that? Wouldn't your wife be disappointed if you go back to work?"

"I'd have to ride every ship in the line to do my work well, and I'd need a very competent secretary. Ideal jobs for me and Joyce, believe it. Both of us got a hoot out of nearly all of this trip, and we wouldn't mind if the trips went on for years.... Well, think it over, Captain. Talk to your people, and let me know what the decision is. Me and Joyce will be at home waiting, for a while at least."

MELVIN, THE VAMPIRE

"You're a Shakespearean actor and I've pulsed strings to get you a good chance for playing *Hamlet*," Galen Flornoy boomed happily. "I know it's a rock-and-roll version of the property, but they'll keep the monologues by writing rap numbers for you to do. Believe it, Stevie Spielberg swears you'll be great, and there's nothing I can add to that."

Flornoy was shrugging massively when he put down the office phone and glanced at the newcomer in his office. "You can't make an actor happy. I give that dude a chance to play *Hamlet* for Disney instead of in a cockamamie stage show in Deerfield, Minnesota, and he wants to make waves."

"Your commission for even a bizarre film like that is a lot higher than for a stage show that's faithful to Shakespeare and he knows that." Flornoy's niece pointed out.

"Well, he won't go against his agent's 'suggestion.' No actor would dare fight an agent."

His niece shrugged, causing Flornoy to glare. She had been sent to him by his older sister to learn the dramatic agent business. Been wished on him was more like it. Been inflicted on him, like a root canal.

Nikki Winthorp had turned out to be a cynical twenty-something, not bad-looking in the proper light, who saw a lack of ethics in every move or gesture made by her hard-working uncle. Flornoy had even put her on the payroll when she arrived two weeks earlier, although at the lowest wage he had ever offered for somebody in an entry-level position, but felt like he was paying a lawyer on the other side.

He took his next call on his office cellular phone, stamping up and down the fragile carpet while short-changing a writer client. He swore he had got the best possible sale price for the writer's unproduced play, but was buying it himself under a different name and was sure he'd be selling it in turn to the Time Warner honchos at a much heftier price.

"I don't think that's ethical," Nikki was saying almost before he broke the connection.

This girl might become a source of trouble even if the client hadn't heard her. What of other clients? Not for nothing was Galen Flornoy known to his New York colleagues and to Hollywood visitors as the tiger shark's tiger shark. Unlike Hamlet, he promptly decided to take arms against a sea of troubles and, by opposing, end them.

"I've got an errand for you," he said, thinking only about getting this chickie out of his thinning hair. "I want you to look through the want ads in *Daily Variety* and follow up the first one that seems promising. For instance...*here's* the one. 'Need writer for very unusual non-fiction book that will make a fortune.' Go into the nearest vacant office, call the phone number, and make an appointment to see him or her."

"Even if I have to go to California?"

Especially. "Find out how much he'll pay for the job. Do that when you see him or her."

"But I have to say I'm not a writer."

"Just say you represent the agency, and if this rube will go high enough we'll give the job to one of our writers."

"I'll let you know the situation as soon as I come off the phone."

"Don't bother—uh, I trust you, honey."

* * * * * * *

He happened to be doing dinner that night with Cedric Quix, the action film star who was seriously interested in a project that would use three actors in Flornoy's stable. Hearing that the property was on its twenty-third rewrite and only two more should get it on its feet, Flornoy positioned six of his writers for the job. He and Quix agreed to a cheap unit price for everybody because Flornoy, in exchange, would become a no-show executive with points in the star's production company. They were centering down on a price when Flornoy felt himself being tapped twice on his weak shoulder.

Instead of a fish-eyed waiter, he was staring at his suddenly radiant niece. Nikki's eyes gleamed, her cheeks and even the tips of her ears were Indian-red

October weather couldn't explain the girl's eager-puppy attitude.

"Uncle, it's wonderful and I can't thank you enough for putting me on this job."

"See me tomorrow morning at the office," he snapped, and turned back brusquely to Quix and the nearly-done deal. He would take measures to keep her far from him in the future. What are vice-presidents for?

"But don't you understand, Uncle?" Nikki persisted. "The book will be the first person story of—"

Flornoy excused himself again to Quix, ignoring the actor's hurt ego at not having been recognized. "How much is this idiot willing to pay a writer-client of ours?"

"We didn't talk about that."

"I told you to talk money to him before coming back to me."

"But you don't realize that it's going to be a great true, almost human document. It's strongly supernatural."

There was an interruption from Cedric Quix, whose attention had been firmly caught, which saved Nikki from having her head doused viciously in cock-a-leekie soup.

"Supernatural?" the actor mused. "I've been looking for something that'll get me away from the action stuff, and a fact-based supernatural story could be just the ticket: sincere, emotional, deeply moving, and full of blood and gore and special effects."

* * * * * * *

Flornoy spent his time from midnight to dawn with a singer whose agency contract's extension depended on her performing some services that hadn't been written down. Tired but happy when he dragged himself to work the next mid-morning, he decided to pace himself over the next twenty hours or so.

He had to talk to Nikki about the deal which, at least temporarily, had caught Cedric Quix's ever-wandering interest. As her boss, it was easy to keep Nikki on the other end of an inter-office phone, he had decided. If she argued, he could always hang up on her.

It seemed that the ad in yesterday's *Daily Variety* had been taken out by Stefan Mielnik, a man born under a different name in far-off Transylvania and exiled to Poland, where he had arrived during the reign of King Jagiello.

"A king of Poland? You must be putting gravel in your milk."

"Stefan Mielnik is thousands of years old," Nikki said solemnly, putting the meat of the matter down on her uncle's plate. "He is a vampire."

Over Flornoy's brief but impassioned prayer to Loki, the god of dramatic agents, his niece explained that Mielnik had been able to reach America only after the Iron Curtain had fallen, and now planned to earn a fortune through a book about his long, long life and times.

"I'll go see him and get him to sign an agency contract...no, Nikki, you don't have to bother yourself by coming with me. Soon as his "X" is on the paper, I'll let you take over and see the deal through."

Telling himself that more and more sickies were getting into branches of show biz and overwhelming the sickies who were already established, Flornoy phoned the number that his niece had given him earlier.

...And heard a hesitant, foreign-accented voice: "You have reached Stefan Mielnik. I cannot come to the telephone now, but if you leave your name, phone number and message after you hear the beep, I will get back to you after sundown."

Those last two words cheered Flornoy up, convincing him that the prospective client could make a desirable impression. This calculating dweeb would deserve everything he got from the Galen Flornoy Agency, and he'd be getting plenty.

Flornoy left only his name and said he'd be visiting at eight p.m. He wished he could have sent the writer Anne Rice instead, but she had not put her signature on his agency contract.

* * * * * * *

"You claim you've been dead for a long time," Flornoy said crisply, less than a minute after coming face-to-face with his target. "Do you think you can face out anybody except Nikki Winthorp with a mess of clams like that?"

"I have no defense but the truth."

"If you're a vampire, how come I see you in that mirror over there?" Flornoy had maneuvered shrewdly in the small room with only that test in mind. "A vampire can't be seen in a mirror."

"This is folk tale about us, intending to frighten people. If *you* can see me, the mirror can."

He sounded sure of himself. Probably a failed actor sagging under a triple dose of Prozac, but he carried conviction. Even his make-up, on such a gaunt customer who was probably in the mid-fifties, couldn't be detected.

Mielnik lived in a small co-op building on Amsterdam Avenue on the Upper West Side of Manhattan. Flornoy wondered briefly if he was chairman of the building's Board of Directors, but decided against asking.

"Do you sleep in a coffin?"

"Certainly not."

Flornoy shrugged. "We can get a coffin in here if the book takes off, and arrange a photo session."

Stefan Mielnik winced at the notion.

Flornoy mused, "I suppose you do live on blood."

"I prefer not to speak of this."

"You better say you do, if you want a Book-of-the-Month selection, a big paperback deal, audio cassettes, foreign sales, a George Romero film and a musical by Andrew Lloyd Weber. And I'm not even mentioning computer games."

"In that case—yes, it is true. I do exist on the—the liquid you have named."

"It's going to make you a mint, though I don't suppose it tastes as good as Snapple." Flornoy folded his thin lower lip between pudgy thumb and forefinger.

"How do you get the stuff?"

"This I will *not* tell. You could hang me, electrocute, cut off my head, and subject me to other inconveniences, but I will not tell."

Flornoy recognized a case of terminal stubbornness when it presented itself.

"All right, we'll say we're keeping that up our sleeves." Which reminded him, not that it had ever been far from his mind. Out of an inside pocket of his winter coat, he drew a manila envelope with a copy of the agency contract geared to hog-tie one more client.

"Here's something you have to sign so that me and Miss Winthorp can be in business for you from now on." He mustered a winning smile. "You pay a writer to do the book—I'll fill in the amount later on, save you time. You get a full ten percent of every penny that the book earns in any form, less the agency's fifty percent commission, of course. Don't think you're not getting a bargain when so many agents are charging much more. Considering a sure-fire property like this, though, I'll make an exception."

Any other actor or con man would have started complaining bitterly about robbery, piracy, aggravated emotional assault and battery or whatever crime he might think of. This one had sunk himself so deeply into the role of an unworldly vampire that he silently reached for the contract, flattened it on the nearest table and picked up a black ball-point pen.

As Flornoy's mentor used to say, both in moments of depression and exaltation, "Go figure!" Go figure indeed.

* * * * * * *

He spent the evening at a well-attended charity affair, the Foundation to Fight Pain presenting a concert by House of Pain. He enjoyed ignoring his beeper summonses and networking with other agents in surroundings that everybody found congenial, so the evening stayed in the plus column.

Hardly had he arrived back at his Fifth Avenue apartment than the phone rang and his niece's clarion voice became lodged in his ear.

"I'm with Stefan and he wants to talk."

So the actor came on, starting huffily, of course. "I have just met a repor-ter."

"And you'll meet plenty more, my good man. Miss Winthorp is putting you on the map so you get a good payoff. Don't forget, we're in business for you."

"I sent repor-ter away."

"Well, it could be all right to play coy one time, but don't try it again. Newspaper reporters are too lazy to use their brains and work, but they can get sore and find out that you owe an ex-wife plenty of alimony back in Chillicothe, Ohio, for instance."

"I cannot permit any of this."

"don't worry, nobody will recognize you under that make-up, which is really great stuff. I was just trying to give you an example about Chillicothe, you know what I mean? Scare you, ha-ha!"

"I want no repor-ters."

"Don't bother to bitch at me, buddy. You're under contract now. If you can get in newspapers you'll be in them and on TV before you know it. Miss Winthorp will be getting you on talk shows. You'll do Conan and Jay in la-la land. Dave and Rosie over here. And we should be able to get you *Sixty Minutes* and maybe even Geraldo. Hey, I can imagine a program's subject now: Men who suck women's blood and the women who love them. Not bad for right off the top of my head, huh, Stef?"

"To all of this I say no."

"By the way, now I think of it, we have to get a handle for you. We need a short but punchy name for newspapers and telecasts to call you, a name that'll be recognized right away. Stef sounds like a girl. Meilnik won't cut it in headlines. Hey, what about Mel? That isn't bad, at all. I like it. Mel, the vampire. Got a certain class. We'll go with that."

"I protest."

"And something else, my man. From now on, you take up your problems with Miss Winthorp. She's in charge of your account and of whatever writer she picks to do your book."

The actor grunted.

"But I tell you what I will do, Mel, and it's a solemn promise." Flornoy knew he had to offer some apparent concession if he wanted the man to take care of his job. "After this is over and the book and the spin-offs are so much dead wood, I'll seriously consider taking you into the agency in a junior capacity. I like actors who are smart enough to play their characters constantly and consistently, and I think that the two of us might get along pretty good together."

Stefan Mielnik showed only a minimum of self-control in the face of a promise that he must have known wouldn't be kept. He sounded as if he had suddenly become sick.

* * * * * * *

Flornoy went about his business, shaving percentages from payments to clients, cutting himself in on deals to which he could contribute nothing except the lowered salaries of certain employees, searching for new deals, making love with his singer friend, and in general living the good life of a New York agent with power over others.

He didn't give a thought to Mel, the vampire, until he saw the papers a week afterward.

He had been on the phone to arrange his first luncheon with Harry Evans at Elaine's when an office boy brought the papers to him. The *Post* headline was: "Vamp Till Ready." The *News* was satisfied with: "We Knew It Would Happen." Anybody wanting to know what that was all about had to turn to the *Times*, and it could take hours to find a particular item on Landfill Wednesday, or whatever today's special section might be called.

Flornoy dug in and found out. It seemed that Mel, the vampire, now called Melvin because of somebody's stupid mistake, had been interviewed unsatisfactorily, and followed out at night by several vengeful reporters hoping to see him attack some stranger for blood. Melvin had lost them.

Tracking the story over the next days, Flornoy wasn't at all surprised when the *Times* acknowledged austerely that no corpses with blood sucked out of them had been found during the entire history of the United States, at least so far as was known on West Forty-Third Street in Manhattan.

With the story appearing in newspapers around the country, it was only a matter of time before boob tube news cameras would pick up on it. A day after Melvin made headlines, cameras from two news shows photographed him from a distance as he left his apartment building for the night and was lost to view.

With the fresh coverage in mind, Flornoy phoned California and the home of Cedric Quix, the star of many action movies. Talking with Cedric would be more effective than faxing him; it was impossible to be sure whether Cedric could read.

"My niece will be calling you very soon about your closing a deal for rights to the vampire story."

Cedric Quix didn't sound as if he had waked up only minutes ago, but he was confused. "What vampire story?"

Patiently, congratulating himself for not having faxed, Flornoy reminded the actor about their recent dinner in Manhattan and Quix's sudden keen interest in a true story about the supernatural. Which, as it just so happened, the Flornoy Agency was handling.

"We've got yards of publicity and there'll be plenty more until the book becomes your next picture."

"My next picture is all set," Quix said. "My production company, Murder Incorporated, is closing for rights to do a re-make of *The African Queen*."

"What? You mean the Katie Hepburn and Bogie wheezer from the year one?"

"A writer was recommended to me without charge by your niece, and helped me come up with a creative twist on the property," Quix said with undiluted enthusiasm. "In my new version, it's the girl who is the skipper of a rundown barge in Africa, salty-talking but good-hearted like Bogie—you know? And I'll play the missionary she rescues, very warm, very sensitive."

The damn fool paused, waiting for congratulations.

Flornoy, even though he was cursing his niece and Quix in not-too-subdued whispers, had the presence of mind to arrange for three of his actors to be cast and enough different writers hired to do at least eighteen of the inevitable re-writes, all at a "sensible" price, as Quix added alertly. For ten minutes after putting down the phone, Flornoy sat in place and swore a blue streak.

* * * * * * *

A publishing friend of long standing, who used Flornoy's invaluable help in preparing royalty account statements to be sent to his authors, mentioned the Melvin situation without being asked.

"You won't get a deal on the vampire story if Cedric Quix has turned it down," the publisher remarked, musing over a chunky panatela cigar and a glass of the best Chablis. "I doubt if you'll get a book from it, either. I won't publish it, and there's no depth to which my firm won't sink in putting out new so-called non-fiction."

"Yes, I'm pretty sure about all that, now," Flornoy agreed. "There'll be no real money from that client."

"Must be a big disappointment to your niece."

"Hell with her," Nikki's uncle said unconcernedly.

She would surely be kept out of her uncle's business if she remained occupied with Melvin. That broken-down actor was still under contract, and she'd be his rep, his only rep. It didn't matter if he hadn't made the cut as long as his many and various problems kept Nikki busy.

It occurred to him a while later, while dickering with some suit from Lorimar, that he might be exposing his niece to a potful of danger if Stefan Mielnik d/b/a Melvin, was a real nut-cake, a creature who might give new meaning to that well-honed phrase, "toxic rela-tionship."

But he told himself not to worry. A girl who could drive a hard-shelled agent to picking straws out of his few remaining hairs must be able to deal with the likes of a mediocre actor at liberty and trying a new gimmick, an actor who was only out to make a greasy buck. If Flornoy was blessed with any sense of reality (and he certainly was) he would feel sorry for the likes of Mielnik no matter what problems he might have. Mielnik was the one who ought to be rescued.

Feeling better, he spent a night on the town and with a new female client, an exotic dancer. By morning, a little groggy, he only remembered that he'd been worried about something on the previous day, but it couldn't have been important.

One of the agency vice presidents, a former errand boy whose father could spare good money in hopes of advancing the career of a son who might have been more usefully employed at the post office, brought in his coffee next morning.

"Is Nikki Winthorp in the office?" was Flornoy's greeting.

"I saw her at the coffee wagon."

"Tell her that from now on until further notice, I want her to be with Melvin the Vampire whether he's working on his book or not. She's to be at his side every minute while he's awake."

"All right, sir."

"Plus which, I want her to know that she can report only by fax or phone or even snail mail, but she's to report only to you and not reach the agency again until she's had a response. She can use any way to get in touch except by personal appearance. Got all that?"

"Yes, *sir!*"

Now that Flornoy had decided Melvin was financially challenged and publicity would be useless, he saw Melvin's name on several news stories. The name appeared almost as commonly and surprisingly as the existence of tanning salons in tourist-oriented sections of Florida.

From a local news show on the tube he found out that some idiot teenagers had waited until Melvin came hesitantly out of his building, Nikki a few paces behind, and poured a bucket of bright red paint over him. Covered from head to foot, the diffident vampire had run back pell mell to the safety of his apartment. He behaved even more newsworthily three nights later. Just as Melvin was leaving a restaurant, where he had given an awkward speech to a little group of serious thinkers named the Horror Writers of America, a reporter asked if it was true that Melvin obtained blood for drinking from the Global Search Blood Bank of Secaucus, New Jersey. Instead of facing down that reporter by spin-doctoring a lie, like any depraved rake of vampire legend would have done off-handedly, Melvin looked terrified and ran off without answering.

With one exception, the media downplayed Melvin's latest caper. The *Wall Street Journal*, not missing an opportunity to reinforce that message its constant readers must have known by heart, wrote an editorial about blood banks. "Will the business opportunity for blood banks to sell to vampires be curtailed," the writer asked plaintively, "by the evil of government intervention?"

Given a client who couldn't cut it with professional help, the *WSJ* had tried sailing to his rescue. Where was the voice of Wall Street when the Flornoy Agency was peddling successful clients?

* * * * * * *

"Are you telling me that Miss Winthorp has tried to get in touch with me?" an incredulous Flornoy demanded of his third vice president. "I gave specific orders that she wasn't supposed to reach me directly, and in spite of that the nuisance phones a few times and asks for me—is that what you're telling me?"

"Yes, sir," the hapless menial said. "She told me to let you know that a recent story in some business paper is making it possible to get even more publicity for our client, this guy Melvin."

Flornoy was too sore to clue the kid into the news that publicity wouldn't pay off for the so-called vampire now word was out that the story of his life wasn't going to bring in money from a movie sale on the Left Coast. Melvin was out of it.

"Should I tell her anything next time I hear from her, Mr. Flornoy?"

"Don't wait for that. Get in touch with Nikki Winthorp right away and tell her to be in my office at exactly three o'clock this afternoon. On the dot."

Flornoy slammed the door on himself when he reached his own office and sat down to give some thought to getting rid of his niece once and for all. He'd been hoping she'd get scared away from working for him after a while spent with that crazy actor who said he was a vampire, but Flornoy had underestimated the hard-working and ethics-driven young woman. It had occurred to him that if anything happened to her, it would solve his problem for keeps. Nobody would be able to say that Nikki's bad luck was her uncle's fault.

Just before three o'clock, when he had decided what to say, it crossed his mind that if Nikki was as much as two minutes late, thereby disobeying a direct order, he would simply fire her for insubordination.

He wasn't that lucky. Nikki not only surged into his office at the dot of three, but she was talking eagerly with every step.

"I've arranged for Mel to get even more publicity, Uncle Galen. He's going to appear at a Barnes and Noble superstore on Halloween for a question-and-answer session about vampires."

"Why would the store want him?" Flornoy asked, startled in part by the affectionate nickname she had used for the client.

"Mel is also going to sign cassettes of vampire flicks. The store thinks it'll make money for them. I know it's not the biggest possible publicity for Mel, but if the agency can arrange nationwide stops like that it's something to keep the ball rolling."

Flornoy was going to snap that it would be useless, but he had never learned to tell the truth to anybody and he held his tongue. Melvin had glided in, looking so blank-faced that Flornoy congratulated himself, for some reason, at having been careful.

"You've done everything that a beginner could do, Nikki dear," he said, forcing a smile to his lips. "Now it's time to turn Melvin's case—I mean, his account—over to another member of the agency, a more experienced dramatic agent."

Nikki looked stricken.

"You'll stay home and wait till I call you for another assignment." *You'll wait forever, baby.* "I'm sure it won't be too long before you're on a new assignment, a more substantial one with a real payoff."

"No!" Melvin said flatly. "You will not pull Nikki away from me, even though I am under contract to you."

There was a growl from Nikki's throat, the first time Flornoy had ever heard such a sound from his niece. "If somebody else was in charge of the agency, this wouldn't happen to a good relationship." She smiled widely, but not appreciatively and Flornoy was struck by the length of her teeth, the baby pink at their tips.

Melvin smiled in turn, but shook his head at her glance. "You have made it plain that you are my representative, dear, for handling business matters I should not even approach."

Flornoy was suddenly aware that his neck had become warm, then icy cold and numb. He felt himself held in place by overwhelming hands. His brain, clouding, told him that Melvin had played on his niece's sense of honesty and ethics, causing her to identify with his interests only because she was supposed to help his career. Flornoy didn't fully realize what had happened till he saw through bleary eyes that Melvin, showing strong long teeth, was smiling approvingly from his place in the chair at least a quarter of the way across the room. Only then did he realize who was draining the blood out of his body.

ACKNOWLEDGMENTS

"The Adventure of the Devil's Father" by Morris Hershman was originally published in *Red Herring Mystery Magazine*, Vol. 3, No. 4, 1997. Copyright © 1997, 2013 by Morris Hershman.

"Silent Treatment" by "Arnold English" was originally published in *Guilty Detective Stories Magazine*, January 1958. Copyright © 1958 by Crestwood Publications; Copyright © 2013 by Morris Hershman.

"Choice of Weapons" was originally published in *The Man from U.N.C.L.E. Magazine*, [January?] 1968. Copyright © 1968 by Leo Margulies Publications; Copyright © 2013 by Morris Hershman.

"Never Too Late" is published here for the first time. Copyright © 2013 by Morris Hershman.

"Danger! Man Behind You!" was originally published in *Sir!*, 1988. Copyright © 1988, 2013 by Morris Hershman.

"Ring in the New" is published here for the first time. Copyright © 2013 by Morris Hershman.

"Melvin, the Vampire" is published here for the first time. Copyright © 2013 by Morris Hershman.